Heathland Hollows

JAMES BRENNAN

ISBN: 979-8-9907237-1-9

CHAPTERS

CHAPTER 1
A TALE OF TWO DEATHS

In the secluded heart of the North York Moors, where the wild heather-clad landscapes begrudgingly embrace the imposing edifice of Ashford Manor, the heavens, draped in a shroud of grey, wept with such a soft, mournful drizzle it might have been mistaken for an English summer's day. It was as if nature itself had slipped into mourning attire, sighing deeply for the late Lord Reginald Ashford's departure to the great bureaucratic office in the sky. A procession of carriages lined the gravel driveway, each disgorging mourners clad in black, their faces etched with a grief so practiced it might have been borrowed for the occasion.

These attendees, paragons of propriety, shuffled towards the estate's private chapel, partaking in a silent ballet of social ladder climbing, all under the guise of mourning. For even in the shadow of death, the rich, with legacies set in stone and wills penned in iron ink, command a performance of loyalty, envy, and avarice, all masquerading as respect and remembrance. Amidst whispered condolences and the soft rustle of silk, unvoiced questions of inheritance darted about like bats at twilight, with fleeting glances revealing volumes of long-held resentments and clandestine alliances. Each nod, each hand clasped, was laden with the history of unspoken words and actions deferred, a testament to humanity's eternal quest for 'something more', or at the very least, a larger piece of the estate.

Despite the grandeur and the high drama, an undercurrent of banality persisted, as if the entire affair were but a well-rehearsed play, the cast all too familiar with their lines. The rich, stripped of their finery and faced with mortality, were revealed to be not so different from the poorest beggar—save for the quality of their coffins.

The sky, having exhausted its tears, watched in somber silence as the mourners huddled under its expansive dome. It bore witness to the grand theatre of grief, as the mourners made their solemn march, the chapel beckoning.

Lady Eleanor Ashford, the bereaved matriarch of Ashford Manor, presented herself with such an air of mourning fashion that one might have mistaken her for a sculpture adorning the estate's grand entrance. Her attire, particularly the black lace veil that cascaded with a grace befitting her station, obscured her features as effectively as the thick fog that often enveloped the moors. This veil served a dual purpose: not only did it shield her from the inquisitive gaze of society, but it also enshrouded her in the solitude that her soul, weary from the storms of life, so desperately craved.

Her posture, unyielding and statuesque, bore the dignity of ancient stone figures that stood guard over the manor, sculpted with care yet weathered by the relentless tempests of time and tribulation. She was, in essence, as much a part of the manor's legacy as the very stones that formed its foundation—sculpted by circumstance, hardened by the trials of a marriage that was as productive as it was tumultuous.

Despite the sternness that her appearance might suggest, Lady Ashford's demeanor was not without its kindness. The years had etched lines of determination and resilience upon her visage, yet beneath the surface, there remained a striking beauty, undiminished by middle age. Her eyes, when they chose to reveal themselves from behind the veil of mourning, shone with the complex light of a woman who had navigated the highs and lows of life with a quiet strength.

Yet, there was a subtle rebellion in her stance, a defiance not of society's expectations but of the tumult of emotions that raged beneath her composed exterior. It was as if she declared to the world that, though she might stand amidst the storm, she would not be swept away by its fury. Her grace and fortitude, much like the manor itself, were testaments to endurance, to the capacity to weather both the literal and metaphorical storms that life might bring.

Into this tableau of grief approached Mrs. Harriet Westbrook, a distant relative famed more for her talent in the art of gossip than any familial affection. She moved with a deference that teetered on the edge of sarcasm, her expression a masterpiece of feigned sympathy.

"My dearest Lady Eleanor," Mrs. Westbrook began, her voice a whisper that carried an undercurrent of insatiable curiosity, "I cannot express how deeply sorry I am for your loss. Lord Reginald was a pillar of strength, a true gentleman. The community shall feel his absence keenly."

Lady Eleanor, anchored in her solitude, allowed her gaze to drift momentarily towards Mrs. Westbrook. Her reply was draped in the coolness of a shaded grove, "Your condolences are noted, Mrs. Westbrook. They are, as always, most... expansive."

Mrs. Westbrook, sensing an opportunity to probe, leaned in, her voice dropping to a softer note. "It is truly a loss that touches us all deeply. He had such a strong connection with everyone, didn't he? It's hard to imagine the manor without his guiding hand."

Mrs. Westbrook leaned closer, her voice dropping to a conspiratorial murmur, thick with the honey of feigned concern. "But, my dear, beyond the veil of sorrow, there are matters of practical concern, are there not? With no sons to speak of, the matter of inheritance is surely a thorny thicket. One wonders, who shall take up the mantle of Ashford Manor? The speculations abound!"

In that moment, Lady Eleanor's patience, as impeccable as her posture, showed the first signs of fray. "Mrs. Westbrook, your curiosity ventures into realms where it has no invitation," she retorted, her voice a silk lasso pulling back the conversation from the precipice of impropriety.

"Oh, but one cannot help but ponder," Mrs. Westbrook persisted, her eyes alight with the thrill of the chase. "The community talks, you understand. A widow alone at the helm—such a situation is ripe for... discussion. And the estate, such a venerable institution, left without a direct heir—"

Lady Eleanor's tone crystallized into the sharpness of cut glass. "The affairs of Ashford Manor are not the grist for the mill of idle chatter. And as for the estate, be assured it shall find its steward in due course."

Mrs. Westbrook, momentarily taken aback by the steel in Lady Eleanor's voice, attempted a retreat into charm. "Of course, of course, my apologies. One merely expresses concern in these turbulent times."

"Your 'concern,' Mrs. Westbrook, is as noted as it is unnecessary," Lady Eleanor concluded, her voice leaving no room for further debate. With a nod that bore the weight of finality, she effectively closed the door on Mrs. Westbrook's line of inquiry, signaling the end of their exchange with the grace and firmness of a queen dismissing a bothersome courtier.

Elsewhere amongst the mourners proceeding from the manor to the chapel, Charles Windham, Lord Ashford's cousin, threaded through the gathering with an ease that belied the somber occasion. His attire, while appropriately dark, seemed to barely contain the undercurrent of ambition that pulsed beneath. The whispers of his recent fiscal follies clung to him, a more faithful companion than his shadow, lending an air of desperation to his charm.

Approaching Elizabeth Blythe and the two young Ashford girls from behind, Charles's approach was heralded by a playful glint in his eye, an incongruous spark of merriment in the somber setting. With the stealth of a cat, he reached out, whispering a quiet "boo!" before producing, with a magician's flair, a small golden thimble from behind each girl's ear. "A treasure for my favorite ladies," he declared with a bow, his voice a whisper of mischief that cut through the day's gloom.

Jenny and Emma, their initial surprise giving way to peals of delighted laughter, accepted the thimbles with the eagerness of those well accustomed to their relative's peculiar brand of magic. To them, Charles was less a cautionary

4

tale and more a bringer of wonder, a welcome reprieve from the rigidity of their usual existence.

Elizabeth, caught between her charge of maintaining decorum and the undeniable joy in the girls' faces, could only muster a softened glare in Charles's direction. It was a look that spoke volumes—disapproval tempered by gratitude, a silent acknowledgment of the light he'd brought to the girls' eyes. "Mr. Windham, your antics," she began, the edges of her rebuke softened by a reluctant smile, "are both inappropriate and... appreciated, I suppose."

Charles turned his attention to Elizabeth, his approach as light and teasing as the breeze that whispered through the manor's grounds. "And what of you, Miss Blythe? No desire for trinkets or tales to brighten the gloom of the day?"

Elizabeth's response, gentle yet firm, was a polite but unyielding barrier to his charm. "My days are brightened sufficiently by the joy of my charges, Mr. Windham. Your... contributions, though fanciful, are unnecessary." Rebuffed, Charles took a step back, his retreat marked by a graceful acknowledgment of her stance. It was then, amidst the shifting crowd, that his gaze found Amelia Rutherford's.

Amelia Rutherford carried the grace of her early twenties with a poise that belied her years. Her hair, a cascade of rich auburn, framed a face marked by a delicate beauty—high cheekbones, a small, straight nose, and deep green eyes that seemed to capture the very essence of the Ashford estate's sprawling grounds.

"Ah, Miss Rutherford, always a pleasure to find a genuine gem amongst the stones," Charles ventured, his voice tinged with an undercurrent of familiarity that flirted with impropriety. "I trust you've been spared the burden of trinkets and tales today?"

Amelia allowed a small smile to play upon her lips. "Indeed, Mr. Windham, I find myself curiously unburdened by such weights today. It appears all the gifts have gone to my young cousins. Or perhaps you have saved the best trinket just for me?"

Charles, undeterred by the polite veneer of their public exchange, leaned closer, his voice dropping to a murmur only she could catch. "Ah, but Amelia, it's the unseen treasures that hold the true value, wouldn't you agree? Hidden gems, clandestinely appreciated."

It was at that moment the chapel doors were opened, and the crowd began to funnel towards the entrance. As the mourners settled into the solemn embrace of the chapel's pews, the air thick with the mingled scents of damp wool and lilies, the service for Lord Reginald Ashford commenced. The gathering quieted, a collective breath held in anticipation of the words that would pay homage to the man whose earthly travails had reached their conclusion. It was at this moment that Reverend William Smythe, a figure surprisingly youthful for the gravitas of his office, stepped forth to the pulpit.

With an air of nervous energy that belied his affable demeanor, the Reverend Smythe scanned the assembly with eyes that flickered like candles in a drafty room. Clutching the edges of the pulpit with hands that subtly betrayed his inner tumult, Reverend Smythe embarked upon his sermon with a voice that, despite its occasional quaver, sought to bridge the realms of the divine and the mortal. His words, though intended to soothe and solemnize, occasionally meandered into realms unintended, his sentences sometimes embarking on journeys as winding and unexpected as the lanes that crisscrossed the countryside.

"In these times," Reverend Smythe commenced, his voice trembling like a leaf in a tempest, "we are called to reflect upon the... uh, singular journey of life, a voyage... erm, that our dear Lord Ashford navigated with... ah, unparalleled zeal." His gaze darted amongst the congregation, seeking an anchor in the sea of expectant faces, each member clinging to decorum like a life raft in this ocean of grief.

He ventured further, embarking upon a tribute to Lord Ashford's... extensive... connections within the community, "A man of... um, considerable... acquaintance, Lord Ashford's... ah, engagements were as diverse as the... er, many flowers across our English countryside." Here, the Reverend's eyes flickered with the unintended hint of scandal, his nervousness peaking.

"As the... er, seasons change," he pressed on, sweat beading on his brow as if he were a farmer under the midday sun, "so too do we... ah, transition from this... erm, mortal coil to... uh, eternal fellowship." The words, meant to inspire, meandered like a lost traveler, reaching for profundity but grasping only air.

Attempting to anchor his sermon in the bedrock of scripture, Reverend Smythe found himself adrift in a biblical maelstrom. "Just as Jonah was... um, swallowed by the whale, so too are we engulfed by our trials and tribulations. Yet, Lord Ashford, in his... er, navigational prowess, charted a course as true as the... ah, Israelites through the desert." The comparison, ambitious in its scope, received only polite nods more a testament to the listers' training than to any enlightenment imparted.

"As the... er, loaves and fishes were multiplied," he continued, mopping his brow in an imitation of labor under a scorching sun, "so too did Lord Ashford's generosity... ah, proliferate amidst our community." The simile, stretched beyond its tensile strength, hung awkwardly in the air, a testament to the Reverend's floundering oratory.

The congregation, for their part, responded with the mechanical reverence of those well-versed in the rhythms of religious ceremony. Their murmured amens and nodded heads were the choreographed movements of societal obligation, a dance as devoid of meaning as the Reverend's meandering sermon.

While the Reverend's voice, laden with solemnity, spoke of temporal grief giving way to the everlasting, Elizabeth Blythe found her thoughts meandering through memories and musings. Yet, she was jolted back to the present by a sudden grasp of her hand and an eager whisper at her ear. "Does daddy have wings now? Thomas says all people become angels when they die, except for the bad ones. And angels have wings," Jenny's voice, barely a whisper, was filled with the curious innocence of her five years.

Elizabeth, with a smile touched by sadness, gently placed a finger over her lips, signaling for quiet. "Shh, my love," she whispered back, her voice a blend of tenderness and restraint. Jenny, the younger of Lord Ashford's two daughters in her care, looked up at her with wide, questioning eyes, seeking reassurance in a moment filled with unknowns.

Seated to Jenny's other side, Lady Ashford observed the exchange with a quiet intensity. Her presence, dignified and composed, anchored her daughters amidst the sea of mourning. The distance that usually marked her interactions with her children seemed to diminish, if only slightly, in their shared moment of loss. Yet, the formality of her posture and the measured grace with which she occasionally reached out to smooth Emma's hair or adjust Jenny's black ribbon spoke of a love expressed within the bounds of her station and the public nature of their grief.

Emma, sitting between her sister and mother, absorbed the words from the pulpit and the whispered exchange with a thoughtful silence. Her young mind wrestled with the gravity of the ceremony, the finality it represented, and the snippets of conversations that fluttered around her like leaves in the wind.

As Reverend Smythe reached the sermon's end, the chapel was filled with a gentle hum of acknowledgment—not for the finesse of his delivery, but for the sincere effort he poured into navigating his wayward path through it. If only, dear reader, we could all be granted such grace in our own meanderings. But let us press on.

As the final notes of "Abide With Me" echoed through the stone arches of the chapel, offering a somber yet hopeful farewell to Lord Reginald Ashford, the congregation began its slow procession towards the exit. Among them was Dr. Henry Fletcher, a man whose physical presence was as pronounced as his professional reputation. His mustache, a lavish expanse of hair, seemed almost a separate entity, commanding its own respect, while his girth suggested a life of comfortable excess rather than the ascetic discipline one might expect from a medical professional.

Yet, for all his physical stature, Dr. Fletcher navigated the crowd with unexpected agility, darting through with the dexterity of a man who had once maneuvered through the chaos of battlefields, not just the intricacies of the human anatomy and the labyrinthine social circles of Ashford. Behind his courteous nods and the veil of professional concern, a cascade of biting commentary flowed through his mind, an internal monologue punctuated with exclamatory observations on the folly and frailty of those around him.

"Ah, the good Reverend," he mused with a sardonic twist of his mustache, a habit born from years of contemplation under fire and in the quiet of his study. "Teetering on the edge of coherence, much like a green recruit on his first day! Ha! Lord Ashford, now taking his eternal rest, whatever celestial voyage may or may not entail, he cannot escape the most fundamental journey of all—back to the earth from whence we came."

Emerging from the chapel, Dr. Fletcher was met with the invigorating embrace of the North York Moors' air, a stark contrast to the cloistered atmosphere of mourning he'd just departed. He preened his mustache with a practiced flick—part grooming, part battle readiness, as if preparing to face down not just the day but any remnants of ignorance that dared cross his path.

"They look upon me with a mix of awe and sheer necessity," he declared internally, his thoughts a parade ground for his own accolades. "The path of science may be lonely but it is certainly righteous. Forward, march!" he motivated himself as he crossed the terrain of the moors, with its sweeping vistas and the stark beauty of its heather-strewn hills.

Dr. Fletcher's journey took him past a peculiar and arresting sight—splashes of red, yellow, and blue—juxtaposed strikingly against the dark, freshly turned soil. The tribute of flowers rested upon a small, almost intimate area of ground, no larger than a modest chest, adorned with a particularly delicate arrangement of wildflowers. This modest patch, otherwise unmarked and devoid of the grandiose monuments that adorned more ostentatious memorials, was poignant in its simplicity. The flowers, though wild, were arranged with a care that spoke volumes of the sentiments they were meant to convey—of love, loss, and the tender memories held for one who had scarcely breathed the moorland air.

It was a scene that evoked a momentary pause in Dr. Fletcher's stride, a silent salute to the unnamed soul commemorated by this natural monument. "Ah, the unspoken elegies of the forgotten," he mused, his thoughts briefly alighting on his own experiences of anonymous burials in distant lands, where the only markers were the memories carried by those who survived. "Salute and march on, for the living must continue the advance!" The flowers, the earth, the silent tribute—they were left behind, receding into the backdrop of his thoughts as he continued onward.

Soon the silhouette of his home began to materialize against the twilight sky. As he mounted the final step to his abode, he paused momentarily to catch his breath and admire the majestic sprawl of his reflection in the hall window. "Charge forth, ye mighty intellect!" he silently commanded himself. Finally, in the solitude of his study, amidst books, papers, and scientific curiosities, the doctor found his sanctuary, a bastion against the follies of the world outside, a world that awaited his return, not unlike the damp ground of the earth that would one day call him back.

* * *

As it so transpires, the mortal remains of Lord Reginald Ashford were, at that very juncture, being primed to heed the solemn summons, in readiness for a last voyage to unite with his ancestors beneath the shadowed embrace of the chapel's neighboring soil. The air, laden with the essence of freshly turned earth and the subdued fragrance of funeral blooms, enveloped the smaller assembly of mourners gathered for the interment. A chilling void awaited Lord Ashford, a gaping maw in the ground that seemed to drink in the light, casting an unsettling pall over the proceedings.

Lady Ashford stood steadfast with her daughters, Jenny and Emma, by her side. The ominous sight of the open grave tugged at young hearts with tendrils of dread, the finality it represented a concept too vast and morbid for their innocent minds to grasp fully. Noticing the shadow of unease that flickered across her daughters' faces, Lady Ashford leaned down, her voice a whisper of silk and steel meant to bolster their spirits. "Remember, my dears," she murmured, a tale of the soul's flight weaving through her consolation, "your father embarks on a grand adventure, one where he shall watch over us, ever present, ever loving." Nearby, Elizabeth Blythe, her role as governess momentarily secondary to that of a steadfast companion, offered her silent support, her presence a comforting constant in the lives of the young Ashford daughters.

In stark contrast to the solemnity of the moment, Charles Windham found repose against the cold stone of a nearby tombstone, his posture one of indolent laziness. This casual lean, a display of irreverence in the face of death and mourning, served as a silent proclamation of his detachment from the gravity that anchored the rest of those present. His presence, though physically among the gathering, seemed a world apart, lost in a contemplation or conceit known only to him.

The Reverend William Smythe, ever the shepherd of his flock, could not help but notice Charles's stark incongruity with the solemn atmosphere. The Reverend's gaze lingered on Charles, a frown creasing his brow as if he wrestled with the urge to chastise. Instead, the Reverend turned back to the gathered mourners, his voice rising in a final eulogy.

"As we commit our beloved Reginald to the earth," the Reverend intoned, "let us remember the bonds of love and kinship that unite us, in grief as in joy." With a nod, he signaled to the attendants to begin the solemn process of lowering Lord Ashford's body into the waiting embrace of the grave.

However, this solemn moment was abruptly shattered by the sound of a carriage careening up the road adjoining the chapel. As the carriage came to an abrupt stop, two uniformed men alighted with an urgency that matched the vehicle's haste. "Halt!" bellowed the younger of the two, his voice cutting through the somber quiet.

Constable Timothy Barkley, as he was known, stepped forward with a swagger that seemed all too grand for his compact frame. A man of middling height, Barkley's build was sturdy, if not slightly rounded at the edges, suggesting a fondness for the comforts of the local pub. His face, framed by a crop of hair that could only be described as obstinately unkempt, was marked by a pair of keen eyes that darted about with an energy that bordered on the frenetic. Below a nose that looked like it had seen its share of altercations, his mustache—a thin line of ambition—attempted to lend a seriousness to his youthful visage. His uniform, though worn with a certain pride, seemed to strain against its duties, much like the man it encased. His voice, when it broke the somber silence, grated against the genteel mourning of the assembly with a roughness that betrayed his East End roots.

"Now, 'old on just a tick," Constable Barkley commanded, his tone rough and tinged with a hint of relish at the authority he wielded. "Right, listen up, everyone!" he announced, scanning the faces before him with an intensity as absolute as it was seemingly unnecessary. "This 'ere is a serious police matter, and I'm 'ere to make sure things go by the book. And what I mean by that, if it ain't already clear as day, is that no one—and I mean no one—is to even think about putting that body in the ground while I'm standing 'ere. Not on my watch!"

His eyes darted from person to person, as if expecting a sudden, collective lunge toward the coffin. "I've got me eyes on all of ya. Especially you," he pointed, somewhat arbitrarily, towards a bewildered Emma, who blinked back in innocence. "I know you're small, but that means you could sneak around easy, doesn't it? Well, it won't work, not with me 'ere!"

The Constable's gaze then snapped to the Reverend Smythe, who had been observing the unfolding scene with a mixture of alarm and incredulity. "And don't think I don't see what you're about, Reverend, with your soothing words and calm demeanor. Planning to bless the ground and make it all official-like before we can stop ya? Not happening! Ladies and gents, this is a police matter now, and that means procedures, understand? Procedures that don't include any surprise burials, not today!"

Barkley continued, pacing a small circle as if to physically encompass the potential threat. "We've got reports, accusations, investigations to conduct! So, the lot of you, just step back and let the law do its work. And I'll be watching, I will. Every one of you, every move."

Inspector Hargreaves, stepping forward with a sigh that seemed to carry the weight of long-suffering patience, laid a hand on Barkley's shoulder. "Perhaps what my colleague is trying to express," he began, with a diplomacy that hinted at frequent practice, "is that we're here to ensure that all aspects of the law are respected. Reports have been made, accusations lodged. We must follow due process."

Tall and lean, Hargreaves cut an imposing figure, his stature accentuated by the straightness of his posture and the sharp lines of his uniform. His face, framed by meticulously groomed hair that hinted at a strict adherence to personal protocol, bore the marks of a man who valued precision and decorum above all. His eyes, sharp and assessing, swept over the assembly with the practiced ease of one who had navigated the tangled webs of crime and justice for years.

"As you know, Lord Ashford was no mere citizen," Hargreaves intoned, his gaze sweeping across the collected mourners with an intensity that bespoke the seriousness of his next words. "Indeed, he was a man who navigated the labyrinthine corridors of administration with the same ease and aplomb with which he managed his estate."

Hargreaves continued, "Thus I assure you that this investigation must and will be conducted with an eye towards not just justice, but towards impeccable procedural integrity. The eyes of the bureaucracy are upon us. Every step, every action we undertake in the course of this investigation will be measured, recorded, and executed with a fidelity to the rulebook that Lord Ashford himself would have demanded. So let's proceed with a calm and orderly—"

"Halt!" Barkley interjected once more, as if the word itself were a shield against the feared onslaught of shovels and ceremony. "No burying, not till we say so. It's the law!"

"Constable, that will suffice," Hargreaves interjected with a look that managed to convey volumes of reproof in a single glance, causing even the impetuous Barkley to take an involuntary step back.

He paused, surveying the sea of puzzled faces still struggling to grasp the sudden turn of events. With a dramatic step forward Hargreaves declared "Ladies and gentlemen, I am here on official police business." He drew a deep breath, his chest expanding as if to draw upon the collective anticipation of his audience, wagging an accusatory finger at the guilt seemingly encompassing the entire heathland, before delivering his coup de grâce with a fervor that echoed against the ancient stones. "We are here to investigate... murder!"

CHAPTER 2
BLEAK HOUSE

In the deep, silent embrace of predawn, Ashford Manor stood as a steadfast guardian over the mist-enshrouded landscape, its stone façades, scarred by time and ivy, whispering ancient tales. This edifice, a testament to the pride of its lineage, held secrets and sins of generations within its unyielding gaze across the estate, obscured by fog like a scene draped in a painter's melancholic strokes.

Thomas Graves awakened to the day's demands with the reverence of a monk to his prayers. His room, austere yet steeped in the manor's history, was a cocoon of servitude. As he dressed, each article of his uniform—a fabric woven from duty and precision—mirrored his dedication in the glass, showing a man marked by the passage of time, silver strands threading through his dark hair.

The day commenced with the meticulous cadence of a symphony, his thoughts orchestrating the household's rhythms. "6:03 AM, the dining hall's silver—its luster must not tell of negligence. 6:17 AM, the east wing's ancestral portraits—Sir Edmund's frame must not suffer the indignity of dust. 6:32 AM, the greenhouse blooms for Lady Eleanor's tray." Graves meticulously planned, his inner monologue a testament to his unwavering commitment.

The day's precise choreography continued as Graves' vigilance extended beyond the polish of silver and the dust on portraits. "6:45 AM, upon inspection of the study, one of the Ashford's small but priceless keepsakes—a silver snuff box, a relic of generations—was conspicuously absent," he noted with a furrowed brow. This wasn't the first item to vanish; a troubling pattern of disappearances that gnawed at him. While he pondered the possibility of a light-fingered staff member, part of him wondered if perhaps the item had been relocated in preparation for Mr. Ashford's service or at the behest of the family barrister. The thought did little to ease his concern, but protocol demanded he reserve judgment and quietly monitor the situation.

With dawn's first light cutting through the night's shadows, Graves ventured into the bustling heart of the manor—the kitchen. Here, the quiet of morning shattered against the vibrant tempest of Chef Henri Leclair's realm. Leclair dominated the space not just through his considerable physical presence, but with the sheer intensity of his culinary passion. Broad shoulders strained against the fabric of his chef's jacket, and his hands moved with surprising grace despite their size. His dark hair, usually swept back in the heat of the kitchen, framed a face where sharp eyes sparkled with a fervor.

"Regardez! This soufflé, a disgrace that soils the name of culinary art!" he thundered, his voice a deep rumble that resonated through the kitchen. The young apprentice before him stood petrified, caught in the storm of Leclair's displeasure. "We are artisans, creators of sublime experiences for the palate. We do not serve mediocrity here!" His French accent lent a dramatic flair to his words, even as his gaze swept over the bustling kitchen staff in warning.

"Precision, mes amis, precision is the soul of our cuisine!" he instructed, his tone softening as he seasoned a sauce with a practiced flick of his wrist.

Graves, on the kitchen's threshold, beheld the spectacle with a stoic air, resigned yet admiring of the chef's fiery passion. Attempting an interjection, he was swiftly enveloped in Leclair's vibrant tirade on culinary excellence.

Navigating his day's litany with practiced ease, Graves continued his itinerary.. "7:15 AM, the breakfast service awaits. May the night's shadows have spared young Misses Jenny and Emma from yesterday's sorrows," he pondered, his steps now leading him to the day's unfolding drama in the dining room.

As Graves entered the dining room, the morning light cast a soft glow over its occupants, revealing Lady Eleanor, Elizabeth Blythe, and the two young girls, Jenny and Emma, each ensconced in their own world of thought. Lady

Eleanor, her voice a blend of dignified sorrow and disbelief, broke the morning's silence. "I hope others fared better than my restless night. I cannot fathom the purpose behind this investigation. We are all reeling from the shock and sorrow of my husband's passing, and yet, to suggest murder? It is beyond comprehension," she mused, her words hanging in the air like a delicate mist.

Elizabeth, ever the embodiment of grace and propriety, echoed Lady Eleanor's sentiments with a measured nod. Lady Eleanor, her spirits ruffled by the audacity of the accusation, continued "The gall, to spirit his body away at the very moment of his interment!"

Jenny, with the unfettered curiosity of youth, posed a question that hung in the air like a chill. "What does 'murder' mean?" she inquired, her voice a mixture of innocence and budding awareness.

Lady Eleanor, seizing the moment to dispel the shadow that had crept over their morning, quickly responded. "Murder, my dear, is a word these policemen use to feel more important than they are. They fancy their roles quite dramatically, you see. They put on their uniform and think themselves in a novel or play."

Emma, her interest piqued by her sister's question and their mother's response, chimed in, "But why did the constable point at me, mother? Was he practicing for a play?"

"Oi, don't you worry 'bout a thing, Miss Emma," Jenny proclaimed with a flourish, her small hands on her hips in imitation of Constable Barkley. "I got me eyes on all of ya, I do!"

Emma, not to be outdone, wagged a finger in the air, her face a mask of mock seriousness. "And you there," she said, aiming her finger at an imaginary culprit with all the solemnity of a seasoned officer, "not one step closer to the biscuit tin without my say-so!"

"Oh dear, it appears I've been caught in a most dastardly act," Graves declared, his voice laden with mock solemnity as he approached the girls. With a conspiratorial glance towards Lady Eleanor and Miss Blythe, he produced two biscuits with a flourish. "As atonement for my grievous misdeeds, I offer you each a biscuit, in hopes of securing your silence on the matter," he continued, bending down to their level with a gentle smile.

Lady Eleanor, observing Graves's interaction with the girls, found a smile tugging at her lips. "Mr. Graves, how long have you now served at Ashford?" she inquired, her tone warm. "Your dedication has always been apparent, but seeing you with the girls today... I must say, it's comforting."

Graves, straightening up but still allowing a softness to linger in his eyes, replied, "It'll be twenty years this December, Lady Eleanor."

Eleanor nodded, appreciating his loyalty. "I want you to know, come what may, we'll ensure you're well taken care of. I hope you'll agree to stay on, even after... everything settles."

Clearing his throat, Graves subtly adjusted his stance, as if donning once more the invisible armor of his professional guise. "Speaking of estate affairs, Lady Eleanor," he began, the words as measured and precise as the ticking of the grandfather clock in the hall, "Mr. Harrowgate, the family barrister, is expected to arrive at 1 o'clock this afternoon for the reading of Lord Ashford's will."

He paused, the brief silence heavy with anticipation. "Furthermore, Mr. Charles and Master Julian have both communicated their intentions to be present." Graves's voice betrayed a hint of unease at the mention of Julian's name, well aware of the undercurrents of tension his presence would invariably bring.

Lady Eleanor's expression cooled considerably at the news, a frost creeping over the warmth that had briefly inhabited her features. "The nerve of that man!" she exclaimed, her voice a mixture of disbelief and indignation. "He did not even deign to attend his own brother's funeral, and yet he presumes to show his face now, at the reading of the will?"

Graves gave a curt but sympathetic nod. "Yes, my lady."

The sudden appearance of the young housemaid Molly Dawson caught Graves off guard, a shadow momentarily flickering across his otherwise composed visage. "Ms. Dawson," he began, "it is good to have you back. Could you kindly inform Chef Leclair that we shall be expecting guests this afternoon?"

Molly paused, her hands momentarily stilling from their task of clearing the table, the clatter of dishes ceasing. She turned towards Graves, offering a faint smile. Her hair, a rich chestnut hue, was pulled back in a simple style, strands escaping to frame settled into a soft, warm expression, yet beneath her eyes' surface, a turmoil seemed to churn. "Oh, yes, Mr. Graves, I'll tell 'im straight away. And, um, thank you, sir," she replied, her voice carrying a tentative note.

Her acknowledgment was polite, yet her eyes darted away quickly, returning to the task at hand with a haste that seemed to underline her desire to blend back into the background. Molly made her way back to the kitchen, the warmth and the clatter greeting her. She found Chef Leclair overseeing a flurry of preparations.

"Henri," she began, approaching the chef and speaking softly, "Mr. Graves says we're to expect guests this afternoon."

Leclair turned towards her, his expression brightening at her approach. "Ah, Molly," he responded, a mix of warmth and concern enveloping his words. "The kitchen hasn't been the same without its étoile brillante," he remarked, his use of French not just a habit but a gentle effort to coax a genuine smile from her. "As you can see, the entire house has fallen into mourning during your absence. It must be strange to return at a time like this. But, how was your visit home? Were your parents well?" Henri inquired, his tone a blend of warmth and worry.

"It was fine, thank you, Henri," Molly replied, her voice low, "the time was a soothing comfort."

"Ah, but you see, Molly," Henri continued, stepping a bit closer, his voice dropping to a tender, flirtatious whisper, "I've always believed that your beauty eclipses the allure of even the most exquisite dish I could ever create. Les yeux comme les étoiles," he emphasized, his French accent wrapping around the words 'eyes like stars,' imbuing them with an intoxicating charm.

Molly's cheeks flushed a soft pink, his words igniting a warmth within her. Henri, noticing her reaction, ventured further with his flirtations, his confidence growing alongside the playful sparkle in his eyes. "Et cette lumière dans ton visage, it outshines the very candles that light this kitchen," he murmured, his gaze admiring the gentle glow of her face. "Your elegance, ma chère, rivals that of the finest wines in our cellar. And your laughter," he paused, his voice a soft caress, "is the most delightful melody, sweeter than any dessert I could craft."

Molly, caught between embarrassment and delight, found her mood lifting, if only for a few moments, in spite of herself.

"So, we are to have guests this afternoon?" Henri remarked, his tone shifting back to the matter at hand. He turned fully towards Molly. "Stay with us in the kitchen for the preparations Molly. Join me. Let's create something special for the occasion. A shared masterpiece. What shall be our secret ingredient?" His eyes sparked with the invitation.

Molly, momentarily caught in the warmth of Henri's words, felt the weight of reality gently pulling her back. Her smile, still lingering from their flirtatious exchange, faded slightly as she pondered his question. The light in her eyes dimmed, replaced by a reflective sorrow that seemed to emerge from deep within.

"I'm afraid our tears would be too salty and ruin the taste," she responded.

* * *

The aged wheels of the carriage creaked and groaned as it navigated the winding path leading to Ashford Manor, its progress a slow march through the veil of morning mist. Inside, the air was thick with the anticipation of the day's proceedings—the reading of Lord Reginald Ashford's will. Seated to each other's side, yet worlds apart in demeanor and disposition, were Mr. Harrowgate, the family's long-serving barrister, and Julian Ashford, the younger brother of the recently deceased Lord Reginald.

Mr. Harrowgate, despite his advanced years, exhibited a composed, almost serene countenance, his eyes reflecting the verdant landscape that whisked by. His hair, what remains of it, has long since turned a distinguished shade of silver, often seen peeking out from under the brim of his customary hat. His attire was meticulously arranged, from the perfectly knotted cravat to the polished sheen of his shoes.

Beside him, Julian Ashford's mood was a stark contrast—his brows knitted in a frown, his lips set in a thin line of displeasure. The true cause of his consternation momentarily found its whipping boy in a matter of personal vanity. Julian, in his middle years, had recently discovered a distinct balding spot atop his head, a blemish on his otherwise carefully cultivated appearance that caused him no small amount of irritation. During the carriage ride made several covert efforts to adjust his hair, an attempt to mask the offending patch from view.

"Mr. Harrowgate," Julian began, his tone laced with the grumpiness that had colored his morning, "I trust you have prepared everything for today's proceedings?"

Mr. Harrowgate turned his piercing gaze upon Julian, his expression a mask of unyielding professionalism. "Is everything arranged in accordance with your late brother's expressed desires and the unassailable framework of the law?" he posed. "Indeed, it is," he answered himself, with the confidence of a man who had spent decades submitting inquiries to jurors and commanding them precisely the answer to return.

Julian shifted in his seat, the plush upholstery of the carriage offering little in the way of comfort against the tumult of his thoughts. The barrister's assurances did little to dampen the storm of unease brewing within him.

As the carriage meandered through the verdant expanses separating York from the North York Moors, Julian Ashford's gaze lingered on the window, observing the landscape's transformation. The spectacle of ancient woodlands merging with the undulating embrace of the moors, punctuated by the fleeting visage of the railway—a marvel of the age, cutting its unyielding path through nature's tapestry—stoked within him a complex brew of admiration laced with a keen impatience.

"Oh, the resplendent march of progress," Julian ruminated. "Behold the railways, those steely conduits of advancement, forging veins of progress that breathe the very essence of modernity into the most secluded of domains. Yes, indeed, the trees, the verdant hills, they possess their quaint charm. But oh, what triumph, what glory resides in the iron tracks and the billowing steam of locomotives! There lies the true testament to human ingenuity, not in these relics of a pastoral idyll but in the roar and the rush of progress. If only," he sighed wistfully, "if only the foundations of Ashford Manor could be laid upon such gleaming tracks, propelling us, unwilling though we might be, into the bright, unstoppable future."

The carriage's steady clip-clop rhythm seemed to Julian a mocking echo of the relentless march of time, a reminder of opportunities lost to the obstinate refusal of his brother, Reginald, to embrace change. "Reginald, dear brother," he pondered with a sigh, "your devotion to the past was as commendable as it was misguided. Where you saw preservation, I saw stagnation; where you placed tradition, I envisaged innovation."

As the carriage wound its way closer to Ashford Manor, Julian's gaze fixed on the familiar, yet suddenly daunting, outline of the estate through the window. Its towers and turrets, bathed in the soft light of dawn, stood as silent sentinels to the generations of Ashfords who had walked its halls—a lineage now resting precariously on his shoulders.

He was, by tradition and blood, the heir apparent to this grand legacy, a position affirmed by centuries of family custom that favored male succession. Yet, as the manor loomed larger with each turn of the carriage wheels, Julian couldn't shake the nagging suspicion that Reginald's final years, influenced increasingly by Eleanor's whispers, might have seen a deviation from this time-honored path. The strain between the brothers had only deepened, a chasm widened by differing visions for the estate and by Julian's growing sense of alienation from decisions made within its walls. The possibility that Reginald, swayed by Eleanor or perhaps by his own reevaluation of family ties, might have altered the traditional course of inheritance weighed heavily on Julian. Such a break from precedent not only threatened his direct claim but hinted at a future in which his authority and plans for the manor could be fundamentally undermined.

As the carriage traced its final arc towards Ashford Manor, Julian couldn't contain his unrest, his tone heavy with insinuation. "Terrible, the notion of Reginald being murdered. Unthinkable, yet perhaps not entirely surprising given his nature to trust too freely. And yet, here we are, proceeding with the will's reading amidst such turmoil. Recall, you mentioned Reginald had intended to alter his will the very day after he met his untimely end."

Mr. Harrowgate, his keen gaze never wavering from the leather-bound documents cradled in his lap, addressed Julian's concerns with his deliberate, measured cadence. "Is it tragic, the untimely demise of Lord Reginald? Most assuredly. Does this tragedy cast a shadow of doubt and speculation upon the circumstances of his passing? Indeed, it does. Yet, where does my duty lie amidst these swirling mists of conjecture and suspicion?"

He paused for a moment, allowing the weight of his questions to hang in the air before continuing, "In the execution of Lord Reginald's expressed wishes, as meticulously outlined within the pages of his last testament. Is it within the jurisdiction of law enforcement to unravel the tangled skein of his demise? Without question. Should the procedural sanctity of the will reading be postponed on the wings of speculation? I posit that it should not."

Mr. Harrowgate's voice brooked no argument. "To delay would be to venture into the realm of the hypothetical, a domain fraught with uncertainty and devoid of the solidity of legal precedent. What, then, is our course of action? To proceed, as Lord Reginald himself would have doubtlessly enjoined, with an eye firmly fixed upon the tenets of his legacy and the immutable laws that govern our proceedings."

To this, Julian Ashford gave no response save his silence and a renewed aggressive effort to adjust his hair.

As the carriage came to a gentle stop before the manor, the imposing silhouette of the estate against the morning sky seemed to echo the solemnity of Mr. Harrowgate's words. Julian, taking a deep breath, sought to gather his composure, his hands automatically smoothing over the fabric of his suit and the stubborn patch of thinning hair atop his head. Stepping out into the crisp air, he was momentarily caught by the grandeur of the manor's entrance, its familiar stonework a silent testament to the generations of Ashfords who had passed through its doors.

Their approach was noted by Thomas Graves, who awaited them with the quiet dignity that characterized his service to the Ashford family. "Mr. Ashford, Mr. Harrowgate," he greeted, his voice a soft echo in the vastness of the entrance hall. "If you would follow me, everything has been prepared in the drawing-room for the reading of the will. Mr. Charles has already arrived."

The mention of Charles already being present sparked a flicker of annoyance in Julian's eyes, quickly masked by a nod of acknowledgment to Graves.

Julian and the barrister followed Graves into the drawing room. At the room's heart, Lady Eleanor Ashford positioned herself with a deliberate centrality, her posture as composed as it was commanding, a stark contrast to the palpable tension emanating from Julian, who sat rigidly, his accusatory glances, particularly towards Lady Eleanor, cutting through the silence. Charles Windham, in stark deviation, slouched in his seat, a drink in hand, affecting an air of detachment that was perhaps nevertheless too self-aware.

Mr. Harrowgate presented the sealed will with a degree of solemnity that spoke of decades in service to the law and the Ashford family. It was then that Lady Eleanor, her voice laced with a mixture of incredulity and assertiveness, broke the tension. "Mr. Harrowgate," she began, "have you ever heard of such a thing as a body being taken before burial? And more to the point, do you think you could arrest that constable and inspector for their impudence?"

The question, delivered with earnest gravity, hung in the air for a moment as Mr. Harrowgate, momentarily caught off guard, peered over his spectacles with an expression that wavered between amusement and contemplation. "Madam," he finally responded, "does the law vest me with many powers? Most assuredly. But is the power to arrest police officers among them? I fear not."

Mr. Harrowgate then took hold of the sealed will. The attendees watched as he broke the wax seal—a dramatic flourish to herald the unveiling of Lord Reginald Ashford's final wishes. With the seal now broken, Mr. Harrowgate unfolded the document, cleared his throat, and began to read:

"In the esteemed name of Lord Reginald Ashford of Ashford Manor, it is with due solemnity that his final testament is hereby proclaimed, as set forth with the seal of his hand and heart, in this year of our Lord:

*I. **Bequest to the Eldest Daughter, Miss Emma Ashford:** To my beloved daughter, Emma, I bequeath the bulk of my estate, lands, and holdings, this inheritance to be conferred upon her marriage to a suitor of suitable standing, character, and affection, as judged meet by her loving mother, Lady Eleanor Ashford. Until such blessed union, stewardship of said estate shall rest with Lady Eleanor, to manage, nurture, and protect as her own."*

At the mention of the bulk of the estate going to Emma, under stewardship until her marriage, Lady Eleanor's face softened with a murmur of satisfaction, her posture straightening as if the words themselves fortified her resolve. Charles Windham, leaning back with an air of practiced nonchalance, couldn't resist a quip, "Well, at least someone's future is looking rosy—marriage prerequisites notwithstanding."

Mr. Harrowgate continued:

*"**II. Stewardship in Contingency:** In the unfortunate event of Lady Eleanor's departure from this earthly realm ere the marriage of our dear Emma, stewardship of the estate shall transition to my brother, Julian Ashford. It is my fervent hope that he shall tend to its legacy with a hand both firm and fair, guiding it into modernity with respect for its rich heritage."*

At this, a barely muffled snort of begrudging acknowledgment escaped from Julian, whose jaw had been working furiously as if wrestling with an invisible piece of meat during the reading, his eyes ever darting back towards Lady

Eleanor to fix an accusatory stare.

"Shall I continue without further interruption?" queried Mr. Harrowgate to the room. "A resounding yes." He once again cleared his throat and proceeded:

"III. Bequest to the Younger Daughter, Miss Jenny Ashford: To my cherished daughter, Jenny, I bequeath the charming parcel of land known as Meadowbrook Cottage, with its surrounding acres, ensuring her a residence of comfort and independence upon her marriage, as befits her gentle spirit and Ashford blood.

IV. Provisions Regarding Specific Personal Property:

- *To my brother, Julian, I allocate specific items of my personal property, including the collection of rare books housed in the manor's library and investments in the burgeoning railway companies, symbols of progress and intellect he so values.*
- *To Charles Windham, akin to a son in the affection he has garnered from my heart and his years spent under our roof, I bequeath my collection of prized stallions in recognition of his potential and the bond we share.*

In witness whereof, I have hereunto set my hand and seal, entrusting my earthly affairs to those who remain, with a heart full of hope for their future felicity and the enduring legacy of our name.

Lord Reginald Ashford"

As Mr. Harrowgate concluded, Julian's jaw continued to struggle mightily. "Do my contributions merit mere footnotes?" he couldn't help but mutter under his breath, the words laced with venom.

"Don't take it so to heart, old chap," Charles offered. "It could always be worse. You could have been bequeathed a stable of what I suspect are aging, probably sickly, formerly prized stallions. Fancy a trade?" His smile was all teeth, the kind that spoke of amusement found in the discomfort of others.

Lady Eleanor, her patience frayed like the edges of a well-worn tapestry, interjected with a mix of exasperation and authority. "Look at you lot! Bickering over the remnants of the estate while my husband lies yet unburied. He would be rolling in his grave if the police saw fit to let him rest in one. Have you no shame?"

And so, beneath the portraits of ancestors whose eyes seemed to follow the drama with a disapproving gaze, the drawing room became a tableau of the fate that eventually befalls all great estates when inheritance comes into play.

Mr. Harrowgate, ever the emblem of professionalism, and sensing that good sense dictated a hasty exit, rose with the dignity befitting his years and station. "Is there anything further required of me today but to bid you all farewell and take my leave? The answer, I find, is a resounding no." With that, he gathered his documents and declined Lady Eleanor's protestations that he should at least stay for the prepared luncheon, his departure as punctuated and final as an exclamation mark at the end of a particularly contentious sentence.

In the aftermath, Julian, in a tempest of apparent dental attrition and follicular frustration, and realizing that he was for the moment stranded until another carriage was summoned, turned such a vivid hue of purple that onlookers might well have suspected he was in mortal battle with a particularly resistant morsel of flesh indeed.

CHAPTER 3
DEAD AS A DOORNAIL

In the heart of York, many miles removed from the pastoral serenity and historic whispers of the North York Moors, Julian Ashford resided in his element—a grand bureaucratic office that spoke of power, progress, and a peculiar penchant for paperwork. Here, amidst the many cobblestone streets, the throng of civil servants, and the relentless ticking of the clock, Julian held court as the esteemed Chief Administrator of Railways and Societal Advancement. It was a title so laden with importance and so entangled in the vines of verbosity that it demanded a moment of silence each time it was pronounced. Surrounded by the testament of his progress—maps and charts documenting the iron veins charting the future across England—he sheltered under his fashionable hat, a bulwark against both the elements and the indignities atop his head.

His pride in his department was unmatched, his desk a battlefield of pamphlets championing the march of progress, a term so beloved it could have been his crest. "Progress," Julian proclaimed, "is civilization's heartbeat!" His favorite word resonated through the corridors of power, a mantra that both inspired and, at times, bewildered his colleagues. His role was at the epicenter of an era that saw railways not merely as means of transport but as ironclad heralds of progress. "The Administration of Railways and Societal Advancement," he would articulate, each syllable dripping with the pride of a man who believed himself to be an architect of the future, "is the beacon that guides this great nation towards its manifest destiny!"

As Julian reflected on his illustrious career, his thoughts inevitably veered towards his brother, Reginald. Despite their shared bloodline, their paths had diverged drastically. Reginald, too, had managed to secure his own honorary title within the cogs of government—the Distinguished Conservator of Historical Landmarks and Cultural Heritage—a role that, while respectable, plainly paled in comparison to the tangible impact of Julian's work. Reginald's heart remained firmly rooted in Ashford Manor and the untamed beauty of the North York Moors, his life a testament to the inheritance of an eldest son.

"Progress," Julian mused, a smirk playing at the corner of his lips, "How differently the word resonated between the halls of our offices. He championed the old, the unchangeable, clinging to the past with a fervor matched only by my drive towards the future. Yet, who has truly left a mark? The Chief Administrator, mingling with members of Parliament and shaping the nation, or the Lord of an estate, whose legacy fades with the turning of the seasons?"

"Reginald started with a mansion and a title, and what did he achieve? A meticulously maintained monument to stasis," Julian scoffed, his jaw working overtime as if to chew through his own acerbic thoughts. The irony of receiving token shares in railways from Reginald—a jest wrapped in the guise of inheritance—was not lost on him.

"And to pass over his closest male kin, his own brother, for the stewardship of Ashford Manor," Julian mused, the words leaving a sour taste upon his tongue, "if this is his notion of progress, it mocks the very essence of the term!" The break from tradition in favor of a future tethered to matrimonial prospects—this was not progress. It was an aberration.

Julian's thoughts darkened. "Eleanor," he hissed under his breath. "Her influence, her whispers like a serpent in the garden, are surely the cause." He saw in her not a sister-in-law but an adversary, a rival cloaked in the facade of familial piety.

Julian's thoughts were interrupted when the Senior Deputy of Railways and Societal Progress Documentation and Coordination burst into the office. "Sir, the Constable and Inspector are here, answering your summons."

"Ah, splendid," Julian responded, his eyes lighting up at the prospect of progress. "Show them in, will you?"

Constable Barkley, unmistakably broad and aiming for an aura of command, lumbered in first, with Inspector Hargreaves, the very picture of restraint, trailing close behind. "Well?!" Julian demanded, barely allowing them a moment to find their footing. "Have you arrested her?"

Confusion momentarily clouded Barkley's face. "'Her, sir? You mean..."

"Yes, man, Eleanor!" Julian's frustration bubbled over. "I've already informed you, did I not? It's all in my report. My last visit to Ashford Manor, less than a fortnight ago, was nothing short of auditory warfare between Reginald and Eleanor. The very foundations of the manor seemed to tremble with their discord! And Harrowgate—yes, the barrister—he hinted that Reginald was poised to amend his will, the day following his untimely death. The implications are as clear as day! I expected you to have her in irons at the funeral, hence my absence—to remain untainted by the spectacle."

Barkley chimed in, "Oi, sir, we 'ad a word wif Mr. Harrowgate, right? Though, truth be told, 'e 'ad more questions for us than t'other way 'round. But 'e did confirm that Lord Reginald was all set to change 'is will, specifics of which, mind, your Lord brother didn't divulge."

Inspector Hargreaves sought to add a note of calm. "Mr. Ashford, our investigation is proceeding with all due diligence and in strict accordance with the law. Rest assured that your assertions are being diligently investigated, following all proper procedures and by the book. But I must advise you—"

Exasperated, Julian interjected, "Fine! I have more evidence for you. At the reading of the will yesterday, it was unveiled: stewardship of Ashford Manor falls to Eleanor until Emma's union. The gain is substantial, furnishing her with ample motive to forestall any alteration by Reginald. How do you not see this?"

Constable Barkley's attention sharply pivoted. "Oi, wait just a moment," he interjected, a spark of revelation igniting in his eyes. "You're talkin' 'bout that young'un, Emma, sneakin' 'round the grave, small-like? So, that little one's getting all the money, is she?" His glance towards Inspector Hargreaves was laden with a triumphant "I knew it!" though the Inspector seemed to pay him no heed.

Inspector Hargreaves, maintaining his composed demeanor, addressed

Julian's fervor. "Mr. Ashford, the coroner has conducted a thorough examination of Lord Reginald's body, as per protocol. There was no evidence of foul play, and the preliminary finding suggests heart failure as the cause of death."

Julian, barely containing his incredulity, retorted, "And you find this conclusion satisfactory? Were you expecting to stumble upon a knife still lodged in his back, or perhaps his head caved in? Heart failure, yes, but precipitated by what, gentlemen? Must I elucidate the obvious? Poison! The tool of the treacherous, a weapon perfectly suited to her machinations."

Constable Barkley, ever so slightly off the beat, chimed in with puzzled enthusiasm, "Her? You on about the little miss? The taller of the wee ones, I reckon?"

"No, you daft tool, Eleanor!" Julian snapped, his frustration boiling over. "Now, I implore you, reassess the body, scour it for any trace of poison. Follow the book if you must, but unearth the evidence, solve the murder, and arrest Eleanor! Inform me posthaste upon her hanging!"

As they prepared to take their leave, the Constable and Inspector were met with Julian's final, admonishing words. "Progress, gentlemen! I want progress!"

* * *

Amidst the breathtaking sweep of the North York Moors, a lone figure rode horseback, his silhouette etched against nature's sprawling canvas. Dr. Henry Fletcher, his posture as resolute as his determination, traversed the heather-laden expanses with a purpose that matched the steady gait of his steed. The wind, a silent companion, whispered through the moorland, carrying with it tales of yesteryears and the echoes of a world untamed.

"So, they're summoning the cavalry, eh?" Dr. Fletcher mused aloud, a wry smile playing upon his lips as he contemplated the urgent missive from Constable Barkley and Inspector Hargreaves. "Desperation has led them to my doorstep—or should I say, my stirrup?" His heart swelled with a mix of pride and amusement at the thought. The police, those stewards of law and order, now found themselves in need of his vast reservoir of medical and scientific knowledge. "What use is their so-called investigative prowess in the absence of true scientific inquiry?" Dr. Fletcher chuckled at the image of York's finest, bespectacled and bewildered, reaching out for his unparalleled expertise.

His horse, unfazed by its master's soliloquy, plodded onward

As the doctor neared the boundaries of York, the transition from the natural majesty of the moors to the encroaching embrace of civilization marked a shift in his reflections. "Ah, the blissful ignorance of those who believe the mere act of donning a uniform grants them wisdom," he scoffed. The prospect of consulting with the police on the mysterious circumstances surrounding Lord Reginald Ashford's demise filled Dr. Fletcher with a sense of inevitable triumph. "They may traverse the murky waters of crime and punishment, but can one truly navigate the depths of human frailty without first mastering the atlas of the human heart?"

Upon reaching the outskirts of York, buildings of brick and mortar stood as silent sentinels, guiding Dr. Fletcher's path to the heart of the city. His destination, the York police station, was a somber edifice, with narrow windows peering out like watchful eyes, guardians of the city's peace and order.

Dr. Fletcher dismounted with a flourish that belied his advancing years, his demeanor that of a general surveying the battlefield. "To the fray!" he silently declared as he stepped through the heavy wooden doors into the station. Led down a long corridor, Dr. Fletcher's stride was unwavering. At last, he was ushered into a room where Inspector Hargreaves and Constable Barkley awaited.

Inspector Hargreaves was the first to speak. "Dr. Fletcher, thank you for coming. We appreciate your swift response. As you're no doubt aware, Lord Reginald was under your care. Our investigation into his untimely demise is comprehensive. Meticulous. Thorough. No stone unturned, as it were. Your reputation precedes you, Doctor, and your insights into Lord Reginald's health could prove invaluable. The coroner's initial findings suggest natural causes, specifically heart failure. Yet, in light of certain... complexities...no less than justice and bureaucracy themselves demand that we seek your esteemed second opinion. There is always the chance, of course, that the coroner missed something."

Dr. Fletcher, his chest swelling with a mixture of pride and the thrill of the intellectual challenge, mused internally, "Ah, the coroner's findings wanting, you say? Hardly a surprise. The untrained eye is often blind to the subtleties of the human condition. Yes, the coroner no doubt had went through some education, but was he battle-hardened?" Aloud, he articulated, "Lord Reginald was indeed a man of... let us say, generous indulgences. Worldly appetites. Not the pinnacle of health, by any stretch, and yet, his death was precipitous, unexpected."

Constable Barkley, unable to contain his eagerness to contribute, piped up, "So, you reckon there's something amiss, do ya? Reckon there's a chance the Lord was done in by something sneaky-like? Bit of poison in his porridge, perhaps?"

"Indeed," Dr. Fletcher replied, his voice tinged with the gravitas of a seasoned strategist, "One must consider all possibilities when the battlefield is the human body. The heart, a robust yet vulnerable organ, could indeed succumb to external... influences. Though, when one considers the theatre of human anatomy, all actors must be scrutinized. Indeed, to unveil the full narrative, I must lay eyes upon the scene myself." He tapped his foreboding medical kit with a knowing air, adding, "Fear not, gentlemen, for I come fully armed."

Inspector Hargreaves nodded approvingly. "Every 'i' must be dotted, every 't' crossed, certainly."

It was a short walk to the adjacent coroner's office, with Constable Barkley conspiratorially whispering (sneaky-like) to Dr. Fletcher, "maybe your sharp eyes will catch what our bloke missed," as they entered. Alone, the trio ventured into the examination room—a stark, utilitarian space. At the room's heart lay Lord Reginald Ashford, draped modestly with a linen sheet.

Dr. Fletcher, ever the tactician, approached the table with a measured stride, his gaze fixed upon the form that lay before him. He drew back the sheet, revealing Lord Reginald in repose. The visage of the late Lord, peaceful in death, bore no mark of violence, his features composed as if in slumber. Yet, it was not the tranquility of his face that drew the doctor's interest but the stillness of the chest that once housed a heart known for both its warmth and its weakness.

"The human body," Dr. Fletcher began, his voice a low murmur, "is the ultimate battlefield, where every vice and virtue leaves its mark. Lord Reginald's frame, robust in appearance, belies the internal struggles waged within." He leaned closer, his eyes scrutinizing every visible inch of skin for any clue that might betray an unnatural cause of demise.

Constable Barkley, hovering near the doorway, shuffled uncomfortably, his usual bravado tempered by the gravity of their endeavor. Inspector Hargreaves, meanwhile, stood by with a notebook in hand, ready to transcribe any revelation the doctor might uncover.

"As we stand in judgment over the remains of Lord Reginald," Dr. Fletcher continued, "let us not forget that the mysteries of life and death are often hidden well beneath the surface. Let us begin!"

From his well-worn leather bag, he began to withdraw his instruments one by one, each with a deliberate slowness that seemed designed to enhance their dramatic effect.

First came the scalpel, its blade glinting ominously under the stark light. "This," he intoned, "is the key that unlocks the secrets held within the flesh. A tool of precision, of discernment." His fingers danced lightly over the handle, a master ready to wield his craft.

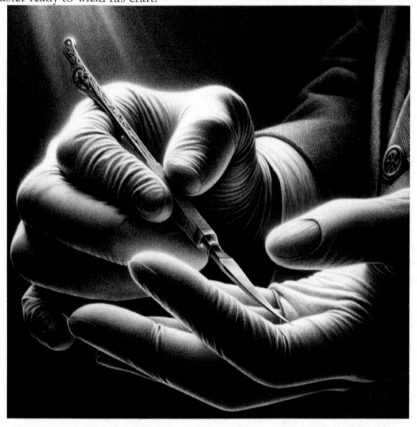

Next, a set of forceps emerged, their metallic limbs cold and unforgiving. "The hands of the investigator," Dr. Fletcher declared, "capable of teasing out the most elusive of clues from the depths of our mortal coil."

Following this, a magnifying glass was produced, its lens catching the light and casting an enlarged shadow on the wall. "The eye," he proclaimed, "that sees beyond what is visible to the naked, untrained gaze. With this, we peer into the very soul of our subject."

But it was the final instrument that drew a collective intake of breath from his audience—a large, needle-like syringe, its purpose as yet unspoken. "And this," Dr. Fletcher said, holding it aloft with a reverence that bordered on the ceremonial, "is our conduit to the unseen, the messenger that probes the mysteries of the blood."

Having drawn the first tool of his arsenal, Dr. Fletcher poised himself over Lord Reginald's body with the scalpel in hand. Arm raised high, the scalpel an extension of his hand, the doctor shattered the silence while bringing the blade down with a dramatic flourish and exclaiming, "Upon this charge, cry 'God for England and the Queen!'"

As the blade made contact, slicing through the cold, still skin with the precision of a practiced hand, Constable Barkley and Inspector Hargreaves exchanged a glance, their expressions a mixture of bewilderment and mild horror. This was not the stoic and solemn examination they had anticipated.

"Observe," Dr. Fletcher intoned, as he carefully maneuvered the scalpel, making incisions that to the untrained eye seemed haphazard, but to him were the choreography of scientific inquiry. "Each cut reveals more than mere flesh and blood. We delve into the very essence of the man, seeking answers hidden beneath the surface."

Constable Barkley couldn't help but interject, his voice tinged with a mix of fascination and discomfort. "Right, Doc, but d'you have to say it quite like that? Sounds more like you're charging into battle than doing a... what's it, an autopsy?"

Dr. Fletcher paused, the scalpel held aloft in midair as he turned to address the Constable's concern. "My dear Constable, we are in a battle—a battle against the unknown. Each incision, each exploration of the human form is a charge against the dark forces of uncertainty and mystery."

Inspector Hargreaves, attempting to steer the conversation back to more professional waters, cleared his throat. "Yes, well, perhaps we can focus on the task at hand, Doctor. Do you see anything that might suggest...unusual circumstances?"

With a dramatic gesture, Dr. Fletcher completed his initial examination with the scalpel, stepping back to survey his work. "Unusual, you say? Perhaps. But let us not jump to conclusions. The body has many secrets to reveal, and we have only just begun our campaign."

"Now, to the heart of the matter," he proclaimed, wielding the forceps with the confidence of a knight brandishing his sword. "Once more unto the breach, dear friends, once more." He inserted the forceps into the cavity created by his initial incision. The instrument danced a macabre ballet within the silent form of Lord Reginald, searching, probing for that elusive truth hidden beneath layers of mystery and flesh.

Inspector Hargreaves, color drained from his face, kept himself busy scribbling notes on a pad. Constable Barkley, his face a mask of both fascination and horror, leaned in closer. "Blimey, Doctor, is that...is that normal?" he inquired, his voice barely above a whisper, as if afraid to disturb the sanctity of the operation.

Finally the forceps emerged, clutched in their grip a fragment of... something. With the solemnity of a priest performing a sacred rite, Dr. Fletcher held it up for inspection. "Behold," he intoned, "what mysteries lie within. Each clue, a step closer to our quarry."

Constable Barkley leaned in, curiosity overcoming his initial hesitation, while Inspector Hargreaves maintained a safe distance. "Observe!" Dr. Fletcher exclaimed, his voice rising in excitement as he pointed to a section of the skin magnified under his glass. "The intricacies of the human epidermis, a tale in every cell!" He moved the glass along, narrating his observations with fervor.

Dr. Fletcher's magnifying glass journeyed across Lord Reginald's body. Each observation, no matter how mundane or morbid, was declared with the gravity of a major discovery. "And here," Dr. Fletcher intoned, pausing over a particularly unremarkable spot, "we might find the key to the mystery, if only the signs would speak!"

"With this lance," Dr. Fletcher proclaimed, elevating the syringe to the light, "we shall delve into the very bloodstream of the matter, seeking out the invisible assassins that lurk within!" Dr. Fletcher carefully drew fluid from Lord Reginald's body while muttering "Through this needle's eye, a secret's told, of deeds dark and actions bold.'"

Inspector Hargreaves watched with a critical eye, pondering the bureaucratic intricacies of documenting such a procedure, while Constable Barkley vacillated between fascination and squeamishness.

"Observe," Fletcher said, holding the syringe aloft, its contents a silent testimony to his thorough examination. "Though this humble vessel may not speak in words, its narrative is no less potent. The secrets of life and death, mingled in a dance as intricate as any courtly masque."

As the exhaustive examination drew to a close, the air in the room was thick with anticipation. Constable Barkley turned to Dr. Fletcher with eyes wide, nearly tripping over his words. "Doctor, that was some proper show, it was! But, uh, between all that poking and prodding and, uh, cutting, did we find our villain, then?"

Dr. Fletcher, placing his instruments back into their leather-bound case with meticulous care, afforded himself a moment before responding. "Constable, the procedure was executed with unparalleled precision and, dare I say, artistry. Yet, the realms of science and medicine demand patience. The samples we've secured this day will undergo rigorous testing. Only time will reveal the secrets they hold."

Inspector Hargreaves, his brow furrowed in contemplation, inquired further, "And of the poisons you mentioned, Doctor—any sign of them?" Dr. Fletcher listed a few potential culprits. "Foxglove, conium, perhaps even the tansy—all conceivable agents of stealthy demise. And there are others as well. But let us not leap to conclusions. The evidence will speak, in its own time."

With a nod to each of his colleagues in science and justice, Dr. Fletcher collected his samples and belongings and exited with a stride that suggested a man embarking on a quest of noble purpose. Left in the wake of his departure were Inspector Hargreaves and Constable Barkley, standing amidst an examination room transformed by their inquiry—a tableau of chaos and curiosity.

The Inspector, surveying the room and Lord Reginald—both in disarray—with a critical eye, turned to his constable with a sigh. "Constable, the aftermath of Dr. Fletcher's, hmm, thorough investigation will require a considerable, carefully annotated, amount of paperwork, I fear."

* * *

As the carriage rattled along to Ashford Manor, the somber hue of the sky seemed to mirror the mood of its passengers. Constable Timothy Barkley, his uniform slightly askew, radiated a mix of eagerness and apprehension, his thoughts a jumble of imagined confrontations and resolutions. The excitement of yesterday's autopsy had barely subsided. Inspector George Hargreaves, however, maintained a stoic calm.

The imposing silhouette of Ashford Manor gradually emerged from the mist. The policemen disembarked the carriage and, as they approached the manor, the constable rapped sharply on the manor's heavy wooden door, each knock echoing through the silent courtyard like the pronouncement of an impending judgment.

The door swung open to reveal Thomas Graves, the Ashford family's steadfast butler. "Good morning, gentlemen. To what do we owe the pleasure of this... unexpected visit?" he inquired, his tone polite yet laden with an unspoken wariness.

"We're here on official police business," Inspector Hargreaves interjected, aiming for diplomacy.

"Yeah, we've got questions for Lady Eleanor, about the murder investigation," Barkley announced, his voice carrying far more loudly and eagerly than perhaps intended.

Graves's eyebrows arched ever so slightly. "Very well, gentlemen. If you would kindly wait in the drawing room, I shall inform Lady Eleanor of your arrival."

As the two men waited in the drawing room, the heavy air of anticipation was momentarily lifted as the door creaked open, admitting a young woman with chestnut hair in a maid's attire. "Would you gentlemen care for some tea or perhaps something a bit stronger to warm you this morning?" she inquired.

Inspector Hargreaves offered her a grateful nod. "Tea would be lovely, thank you."

Constable Barkley leaned forward, his curiosity piqued. "Cheers, miss. Now, between you and me, seen anything odd 'round here? Any reason Lady Eleanor might want to... well, you know, be rid of her husband? Know of any reason for her to be angry at him or anything?"

The color drained from the maid's face, replaced by a rosy flush that crept up her neck. "I... I wouldn't know about that, sir," she stammered, her gaze darting towards the door as if seeking an escape. "I just tend to the rooms and the guests, I do."

At that moment, Thomas Graves materialized at the doorway. "Miss Dawson, your assistance is required in the kitchen," he stated, his tone leaving no room for debate.

With a hurried, "Excuse me, sirs," she quickly withdrew, the tray of refreshments left behind. Graves's gaze lingered on the policemen for a moment longer, before he too once again made his exit.

Some minutes later, Lady Eleanor Ashford entered, still in mourning attire, her presence commanding yet frigid, her greeting to the Inspector and Constable as chilly as the morning air outside. "Inspector Hargreaves, Constable Barkley," she began, her voice devoid of warmth, "we find ourselves in rather...unfortunate circumstances."

Inspector Hargreaves cleared his throat softly before speaking. "Lady Eleanor, on behalf of the York police, I wish to extend our deepest condolences for your loss. It is in times such as these that our duties may appear intrusive, yet they are necessary. Our investigation seeks not only to bring peace to Lord

Reginald but to ensure justice is served, comprehensive and without prejudice. I assure you, any questions we may have, while potentially personal in nature, are asked solely in pursuit of the truth."

Constable Barkley added bluntly, "Right, you're not under arrest...yet." His words hung in the air, earning him a sharp glare from Inspector Hargreaves.

Lady Eleanor, her poise unwavering, responded with a controlled, yet palpable intensity. "Gentlemen, while I understand the necessity of your investigation, I must insist on knowing when my husband will be allowed the dignity of resting in peace. His body should be returned for burial without further delay. Can you assure me that he is being treated with the respect befitting his status?"

Inspector Hargreaves shifted uncomfortably. "Lady Eleanor," he began, "please be assured that your husband's remains will be returned to Ashford Manor with all due expediency, once our... comprehensive investigation is concluded. And I can assure you, the investigation has been—ah—very thorough indeed. Every... ah, piece is being accounted for and meticulously documented."

Constable Barkley gruffly echoed "Every piece!" Then he added, with eyes narrowing, "Per'aps you'd prefer if we didn't examine the body, eh?"

Attempting to salvage the moment, the Inspector proceeded, his questions wrapped in the guise of cordiality yet unmistakably probing. "Lady Eleanor, if I may, could you share with us the nature of your relationship with Lord Reginald? I trust you had a dutiful marriage, but every relationship has its troubles of course. Were there any recent...tensions or disagreements that we should be aware of? We are simply trying to get a complete picture, you see."

Lady Eleanor's posture remained unyielding, her gaze steady. "Inspector, I find the insinuation behind your inquiry to be both inappropriate and unnecessary. Reginald and I, like any married couple, had our differences, yet nothing that would necessitate such...intrusive speculation."

The Inspector nodded. "Of course, Lady Eleanor. However, in our line of work, understanding the dynamics within the household can often illuminate aspects of the case that might otherwise remain obscured. It is with this intention that we inquire, nothing more."

Constable Barkley, however, was unable to resist the prospect of a more direct line of inquiry. "We've 'eard, ma'am, that the Lord 'ad a bit of a reputation for... how shall we say, fraternizing with the fairer sex. Perhaps you found such behaviour... disagreeable?"

Lady Eleanor's composure finally showed signs of strain under the weight of such direct accusations. Her voice, icy with controlled anger, filled the room. "Constable, Inspector, your audacity astounds me. To invade the sanctity of my home, casting aspersions upon my late husband's character and our marriage, is beyond the pale. Gentlemen, it is clear to me now why you are here. You arrive from York, the very city where my husband's brother, wielding his influence, resides. Julian's hand is clear in this. You've been dispatched not in the service of justice but as unwitting pawns in his machinations, seeking to undermine me and further his ambitions for control of Ashford Manor."

The accusation hung heavy in the air, a revelation that visibly unsettled both Inspector Hargreaves and Constable Barkley. The notion that they might be mere instruments in a larger familial rivalry had not previously crossed their minds. Attempting to claw back some semblance of authority, Constable Barkley, his mind racing for a foothold in the conversation, blurted out, "Well, what do you say about foxgluff, connie-um, and, uh, tans-eh?"

Lady Eleanor's gaze sharpened, and she regarded the Constable with a mixture of disdain and pity. "Constable, your grasp of botany is as tenuous as your investigation. If you believe any such substances, however you choose to pronounce them, played a part in Reginald's death, then I suggest you consult someone more knowledgeable than yourselves. Perhaps the local apothecary, if he can spare the time to educate you on the basics of plant life."

Having evidently reached the limit of her tolerance for the day's inquiries, she stood with a posture that communicated finality. "Gentlemen, I believe our conversation has reached its end. I have entertained your questions with as much patience as I can muster. Now, I must insist that you take your leave." Her tone left no room for negotiation, her gaze ushering them towards the exit with an authority that brooked no defiance.

Thomas Graves materialized at the doorway. With a courteous yet firm gesture, he guided Inspector Hargreaves and Constable Barkley through the corridors of Ashford Manor, their exit marked not by words but by the solemn echo of their footsteps.

Once outside, the cool air of the moors seemed to accentuate the sting of their dismissal. As they made their way down the manor's grand front steps, Constable Barkley muttered to Inspector Hargreaves, "Well, she's a sly one, ain't she? Can see where the lil' one gets it from."

CHAPTER 4
GREAT EXPECTING

Now we turn our gaze from the macabre tableaux of autopsies and suspicions most foul to the sanctuary where the light of faith cuts through the early morning shadows and the air is thick with the scent of sanctity and... shall we say, a hint of sacramental wine. Yes, let us retreat into the sacred chapel hall, where the dust motes frolic like wayward spirits in the slanting beams of morning light.

And so we reacquaint ourselves with Reverend Smythe, the shepherd tasked with guiding the North York Moors flock through the valleys and peaks of spiritual life, who recently navigated the tempestuous waters of Lord Reginald's funeral rites. Ah, the ordeal! To orchestrate the final adieu amidst an audience hanging on every tremulous note of his sermon, and then, the abrupt intrusion of the law! Truly, it was enough to unsteady the nerves of the stalwart and the devout alike. And what of the aftermath? Well, our good Reverend sought solace not in the quietude of prayer nor the contemplation of the divine, but rather in the embrace of the vine's liquid bounty.

For, you see, our Reverend Smythe had recently found himself ensnared once more in the comforting clutches of Dionysian delight. A slip, some would murmur, back into the shadows of temptation that had long danced at the periphery of his resolve. Yet, in those silent vigils with naught but his reflections and a chalice of the chapel's finest, Smythe discovered a tranquility that eluded him in the harsh light of day.

In those quiet moments alone with his thoughts and his cups, Smythe found a certain peace. "Surely," he mused, while venturing on another clandestine visit to the chapel's generously stocked wine reserves, "the Lord and His saints would not begrudge a man his means of coping with the trials bestowed upon him."

"Jesus wept," he whispered to himself, "aye, and He drank as well."

Thus we find our Reverend Smythe, not so much fallen from grace as stumbled slightly off the path, indulging in the chapel wine with an increasing fervor that would make a sommelier blush. "To think," he mused with a shudder, swirling the rich, ruby liquid in his glass, "were I a papist, I might believe this very wine transubstantiated into the blood of Christ Himself!" The very notion sent a shiver down his spine, propelling his hand to reach for the bottle yet again. "Blessed are the grape-growers," he declared to the empty room, a toast to his solitary audience, as he poured another generous measure.

With a sigh that bore the weight of both resignation and anticipation, Reverend Smythe took one last, longing look at the nearly empty bottle that had been his silent confidant in the quiet hours of the morning. The liquid had dwindled to but a few precious drops. "To everything there is a season," he murmured to himself. "A time to drink, and a time to preach."

Reluctantly, he set the bottle aside, the final swig of courage burning a path of warmth to his heart. He straightened his robes, the fabric feeling all at once too constricting and too loose, a mirror to his fluctuating resolve. Yet, as he stepped out from the seclusion of his quarters and into the light that spilled through the chapel's corridors, a transformation began. The reverberating footsteps of the arriving congregation served as a call to arms, each footfall a reminder of the duty that lay before him. "Lead me in Thy truth, and teach me," he whispered.

When it came time for the sermon, the Reverend cleared his throat and opened the well-worn Bible before him. "Today, my dear brethren," began Reverend Smythe, his voice steadier than his nerves felt, "we reflect upon a tale of acceptance and divine grace, as we recount the encounter between our Lord Jesus Christ and Mary Magdalene. It is a narrative that beckons us to embrace all, irrespective of their past."

The congregation listened, some with rapt attention, others with wandering minds. Reverend Smythe paused, allowing the weight of the words to settle upon his listeners. Inwardly, he mused upon the faces before him. "Blessed are the open-hearted," he thought, casting a discreet glance towards Harriet Westbrook, the village gossip, "for they shall inherit the truth."

His eyes narrowed briefly when observing Charles Windham lazily stifling a yawn. "For theirs is the kingdom of disinterest, and they shall find themselves wanting when the book of life is read aloud." But his thoughts brightened as his eyes drifted over to Amelia Rutherford. "And blessed indeed are the pretty girls in the third row, for they make the sermonizing all the sweeter."

Refocusing his thoughts, the Reverend continued his sermon. "In the gospel according to John, Mary Magdalene, known to many for her repute, finds herself at the mercy of a crowd quick to condemn. But what of her heart in that moment? Can we not imagine the weight of shame she bore, the silent plea for forgiveness in her eyes as she stood before our Lord?"

He paused, allowing the weight of his words to settle. "And yet, what did Jesus say? 'Let he who is without sin cast the first stone.' A profound challenge, is it not? So, I ask you," he continued, leaning slightly forward, his voice dropping to a near-whisper, "who among us can claim such purity? Who here is without sin?"

The chapel fell into a hushed stillness, the rhetorical question hanging in the air like a sacred challenge. The sudden deep silence caught Reverend Smythe off guard, and he felt a return of his anxiety. He found his wits fleeing like a stray flock. "Indeed, judgment, ah, awaits in expectation for us all, but let us, ah, remember to temper our judgments of others with the grace and mercy we seek from the Divine." He attempted to quickly put an end to the sermon with an ill-advised jest. "Why, if the culprit of our recent turmoil hides in this very congregation, make thyself known! Perchance I'll extend my sermon to our diligent inspector and his earnest constable!"

The response was a symphony of uncomfortable shifts and nervous coughs, the congregation clearly unamused by the notion. A few scattered chuckles did little to salvage the joke from its descent into awkwardness. Undeterred, or perhaps too flustered or eager to notice, Reverend Smythe proceeded to the sacrament of communion. With hands that betrayed none of his internal disarray, he poured the wine with quite the reverence indeed. And then, as he raised the chalice to his lips, the congregation witnessed a draught that spoke volumes of the Reverend's anticipation for this particular moment of divine fellowship.

As the last echo of the morning service faded into the silence of the chapel, Reverend Smythe found himself once more in the solace of his quarters, the sanctity of his own company a welcome reprieve. The morning's exertions, both spiritual and oratorial, had left him with a thirst only the good Lord's other miracle could quench. "Ah," he mused, cradling the bottle of chapel wine like a cherished friend, "if only I could know the divine joy of that first miracle at Cana. Water into wine—surely a sign that even the Almighty appreciates a good vintage."

His reverie was soon pierced by the sound of a timid knock at the door. With a sigh that blended reluctance and curiosity, Reverend Smythe rose to answer the door, his movements languid, weighed down by the inertia of solitude and wine. Upon opening, he was met with the sight of Molly Dawson, her presence a stark contrast to the dimly lit confines of his room. Her chestnut hair, usually tied back with care, now fell in disarray, framing a face marred by the recent tracks of tears and the turmoil of emotions that lingered behind her eyes.

"Miss Dawson," he greeted, his tone betraying a mix of surprise and a genuine warmth that he often reserved for his flock in their moments of need. "This is unexpected. How may I assist you on this day?"

Molly hesitated at the threshold, her form a silhouette of hesitance. "Reverend Smythe," she began, her voice a fragile whisper that seemed to battle with the weight of her unspoken sorrows, "your words this morning... they reached out to me. I felt as if you were speaking directly to my heart. But, I'm afraid I'm... I'm troubled, deeply so."

Her confession, fragmented and veiled in the shadows of shame, lingered in the air between them—a plea for solace from a soul grappling with unseen burdens.

"Please, come in, my child," Reverend Smythe urged gently, stepping aside to grant her passage into his sanctum of reflection and repentance. "Together, we might light a candle in the darkness of your worries."

As Molly stepped into the room, her gaze inadvertently swept across the room, momentarily resting on the bottle of wine that lay almost empty on the table. Once seated, she fidgeted nervously with the hem of her skirt, her eyes downcast, struggling to find the words that might bridge the chasm of her inner turmoil. "I... I don't rightly know how to say this," she stammered, each word a battle won against the silence. "It's just that, lately, I feel as if... as if I've been cast adrift, and I'm... I'm drowning in a sea of my own making. And I fear... I fear that I'm being punished, by God, for... for things I can scarce admit to myself."

Molly's gaze briefly met the Reverend's. She took a deep, tremulous breath, gathering the fragments of her courage. "I...I don't want to speak ill of the dead. But Lord Reginald...he wasn't always kind to me. He was sweet at first, so sweet. And, well, I suppose I enjoyed that. But...but.." her voice trailed off as her eyes darted to the Reverend's wine cup, a silent echo of her unspoken fears. "He was different after drinking. Forceful. We did things...improper things, I am ashamed," she whispered, the weight of her confession pressing down upon her.

Reverend Smythe, sensing the delicate nature of her revelations, offered a gentle nod, his demeanor one of quiet support. "Molly, it is not for us to carry the burden of shame for the actions of others, nor for the situations we find ourselves ensnared in," he began, his voice a soft balm to her churning sea of guilt.

He leaned forward, intending to remind her of the importance of withholding judgment, especially against those no longer able to defend their name. "Remember, my sermon spoke of not casting stones, of not judging lest we be judged. And while it is true," he said, pausing for a moment as he chose his words with care, "that Lord Reginald was known to have his...eccentricities...we must..."

Seeing the distress his words caused, the color draining from Molly's face as if each word were a stone cast against her fragile spirit, the Reverend hesitated. A pang of guilt washed over him, realizing his approach, however well-intentioned, had only served to deepen her anguish. He adjusted course. "But, my dear child, the Lord's mercy is boundless, and His love unconditional. It is not your deeds in moments of vulnerability that define you."

Molly's composure faltered, the brewing storm behind her eyes threatening to break. "But how's I to know God still holds any love for me?" she asked, her voice mingling defiance with despair. "They say the wicked shall be punished, don't they? And truth be told, I can't help but feel a sort of relief, that he's gone. Is it so vile to feel freed from someone who brought you such misery?" Her confession hung between them, heavy as if admitting to the sin itself. "Maybe I am wicked, and maybe I'm just getting what I deserve."

Reverend Smythe, his clarity waning under the wine's influence, endeavored to navigate through Molly's stormy confession with the seriousness it warranted, despite his growing haze. "Molly," he said, "God's love doesn't turn away from us 'cause of our missteps. True, finding joy in another's death is not the way to His heart..."

Her next outpour flowed forth. "I've been punished, Reverend. Lost the baby, I did. Just a tiny thing, innocent as can be...a little boy, I saw him in my dreams, I did. He hadn't done a thing wrong, yet he was taken from me. That's gotta be my punishment from God, for all the wrong I've found myself in."

The Reverend was struck by the intensity of Molly's anguish. He was also struck by the effects of that last glass of wine. As the room spun ever so slightly around him, Reverend Smythe's thoughts began to meander down a peculiar path, his inebriation drawing forth the most curious of biblical reflections, pondering the wisdom of Solomon and babies divided. "Ah, but wait, that child lived," he realized with a hiccup.

Finally, the Reverend ventured, "It's always a tragedy, losing a soul so young. Yet, might there not be a sliver of grace in such grief? The wee one would've grown fatherless." His words hung awkwardly in the air.

Molly's reaction was immediate, her cheeks flushing a deep crimson as the implication struck a chord within her. "Oh, no, Reverend, you don't underst---" she began, her voice a mixture of alarm and caution, and abruptly cutting herself off.

Smythe, his faculties dulled by the wine, nonetheless picked up on her sudden shift. He leaned forward, his expression one of befuddled concern. "Molly, my dear, in these trying times, knowledge could be the light that guides us through the darkness. Did...did anyone else know of your predicament? Your...situation with Lord Reginald, I mean."

Flustered, Molly backed away, her previous openness receding like the tide. "No one knew, I kept it so close, so secret..." Her voice trailed off, her eyes darting away as if seeking an escape.

Reverend Smythe extended his hands and sought her gaze. "Molly, my child," he slurred, his words punctuated by an inadvertent hiccup, "everything...(hiccup)...happens according to God's grand design, mysterious though it may be to us mere mortals."

Molly, for a moment, allowed the warmth of his grip and the earnestness in his blurry eyes to soothe the tumult in her heart. The Reverend continued, "Everything...(hiccup)...will be alright."

* * *

In the resplendent dining room of Ashford Manor, where the symphony of clinking china and subdued murmurs of conversation set the stage for an afternoon teeming with the genteel indulgence of tea and the decidedly less genteel indulgence of scandal, Harriet Westbrook, esteemed local connoisseur of whispered secrets and scintillating tales, had descended upon the manor with the fervor of a sleuth on the scent of fresh intrigue. Arrayed opposite her, Elizabeth Blythe played the consummate hostess and eager accomplice to Harriet's scandalous symposium. Lady Eleanor had absented herself to York on matters concerning the estate, leaving the manor's corridors to whisper secrets in her stead.

Harriet Westbrook, with tresses of brunette coiled with an elegance befitting her station as the village's archbishopess of gossip, navigated the social seas of the community with the grace of a galleon fully aware of its cargo's worth. Her visage, etched with the genteel etchings of a life mid-way through its fourth decade, radiated the kind of assurance only possessed by those who understand the gravitational pull their utterances exert within the orbit of local scandal and small talk. Armed with a vocal range that could easily secure her victory in any sporting event of rumormongering, if such a sport were ever to be sanctioned, conducted her orchestra of innuendos and insinuations with a maestro's flair. Every uttered word, every pregnant pause, was a note in the symphony of speculation she composed with the effortless finesse of a seasoned virtuoso.

While Harriet engaged in warmup exercises for the sporting to come, a similarly passionate drama unfolded at the corner of the room. Emma and Jenny were embroiled in a passionate duel over the custody of a beloved stuffed rabbit, known to all as "Lady Fluff."

"But 'tis my turn, Jenny! You've been hogging her!" Emma's protestations pierced the air, her youthful indignation at full pitch. Jenny, undeterred and brimming with the certitude of her younger years, retorted, "Absolute poppycock! Lady Fluff herself whispered her preference for my company just last night."

"Girls, girls!" Elizabeth chided with a light-hearted tsk. "If you're not careful, Lady Fluff will end the day torn up and in pieces. Perhaps agree to a truce, or it's time for a nap for girls and rabbits alike."

At that moment, Henri Leclair, the manor's chef entered the room, bearing a tray of artfully arranged hors d'oeuvres. Spotting the ongoing tussle, Henri couldn't resist joining in the jest. 'Ah, mes petites,' he exclaimed, eyes twinkling with mischief as he approached Emma and Jenny, 'I see you've discovered the perfect ingredient for my next culinary venture! Rabbit confit with a thyme and rosemary reduction, perhaps? Or maybe a delicate rabbit terrine, layered with the finest herbs from our garden, followed by a rabbit soufflé, light as the clouds above?"

The air, momentarily charged with mock horror, soon erupted into a chorus of laughter, uniting the room in a moment of shared delight. Harriet, with a twinkle rivaling the mischief in Henri's eye, noted Elizabeth's not entirely platonic appraisal of the chef's charm.

Leclair next turned his attention to the two women at the dining table. "Madames, I present to you the latest creations from the kitchens of Ashford Manor," he announced. "Regrettably, Molly is otherwise engaged, so it falls upon me to ensure these delicacies find their way to you directly."

Once Henri had retreated to the sanctity of his domain, Harriet, in the guise of casual conversation, ventured into the realm of inquiry, her questions laced with the subtle acuity of a seasoned inquisitor. "Pray, Lizzie, in these most disconcerting of times, how do you find the tenor of life at the manor? And the lady of the house, our stoic Lady Eleanor—how does she navigate these choppy waters? And the poor, dear children—caught in the maelstrom, no doubt?"

Yet, these queries were but the overture to the magnum opus of gossip Harriet yearned to compose. "Now, onto the matter that has set all tongues wagging—a murderer amongst us! Could it be that our dashing Monsieur Leclair, with his arsenal of culinary cutlery, harbors darker talents?" She paused, a sly smile playing upon her lips. "Though, to be fair, our dear departed Reginald met his end by means less metallic. Nonetheless, a killer with such flair—what a novel thought!"

"Harriet, my dear, we must mind our discourse," Elizabeth chided, casting a glance towards the young Ashford heirs, now momentarily distracted by Henri's parting promise of confectionary rabbits. "Little ears, you know." Yet, her admonition was light, a mere feather on the scales of their conversation, as her own intrigue soon led her to lean closer, voice dropping to a conspiratorial whisper. "But between us," she confided, her eyes alight with the thrill of shared secrets, "Lady Eleanor herself mentioned that the constabulary suspects poison. Imagine, poison!" she exclaimed, imitating the Constable's mangled attempt at pronouncing 'conium' and 'tansy' with a flourish that would have made the man himself blush.

Harriet's eyes widened aghast, her hands fluttering to her chest in a well-rehearsed gesture of scandalized delight. "Poison, you say! How utterly, deliciously wicked! Pray, Elizabeth, you reside within these storied walls; you cannot tell me you haven't a list of suspects tucked away in your bonnet!" she prodded.

Elizabeth feigned a gasp of shock, her hand pressed to her heart as if wounded by the very suggestion. "Why, Harriet, I am but an innocent observer in these grand dramas," she demurred with a twinkle in her eye. Yet, unable to resist the game, she whispered, "But if we're to indulge in the parlour games of suspicion, I've heard it said that sometimes, just sometimes, it's the butler who's done it!"

Harriet clapped her hands together in delight. "Oooh! Thomas Graves! Just the name for a murderer, too!" she exclaimed, leaning in closer as if sharing the world's most delicious secret. "Oh, Lizzie, you are much more of a riot when you're not tiptoeing around the lords and ladies, those stiff bugaboos. And to think, I had pegged you for a proper lady through and through! Delighted to stand corrected!"

Elizabeth waved her off with an affected air of dignity, only barely concealing her amusement. "Well, I never! Harriet, with you as my partner in crime-solving, I wager we'll have this murder wrapped up with a bow before that hapless inspector and his constable even know what's hit them!"

Leaning even closer, her voice dipped into a tone laden with intrigue, Elizabeth continued, "Now, it's been an absolute honor to serve this family, and Lord Reginald certainly had his...let's call them charms, but if we're to be perfectly honest, my dear, the list of suspects in his untimely demise might not be as short as one would hope."

Harriet's expression was a perfect picture of mock horror. "Elizabeth, whatever do you mean? Our dear, departed Reginald, blessed with wealth and standing, had individuals who might wish him ill? Perish the thought! And surely, you haven't a word of aspersion to cast upon your Lady Eleanor!"

Elizabeth's expression softened somewhat, turning to a more somber reflection. "No, not Lady Eleanor," she confessed with a thoughtful pause. "Though heaven knows, the thought might've fleeted through her mind on occasion, given their...complex history. But no, she hasn't the heart for such darkness. Patience is a virtue she wears well, much like her mourning gowns."

Henri Leclair re-entered the room, his arrival heralded by the delicate aroma of freshly prepared canapés. With a flourish that only added to his charm, he presented the latest offerings from the kitchens. "Voilà, mesdames, a taste of France right here in Ashford Manor," he announced.

Seizing the moment, Harriet beckoned to the chef, her eyes alight. "Now, Monsieur, doesn't our dear Lizzie look absolutely resplendent today?" she cooed, prompting a blush to bloom across Elizabeth's cheeks. "Pray, regale us with a description of her beauty, in that enchanting French of yours, if you would be so kind."

Henri, momentarily taken aback by the directness of the request, found himself turning a shade of red that rivaled the finest Bordeaux. Yet, ever the gallant, he rose to the challenge. "Ah, Mademoiselle Elizabeth, elle est comme une rose, radiant and bright, a beacon of elegance in our midst," he waxed poetic, his words carrying the lyrical quality of a sonnet.

Elizabeth, now thoroughly flushed but delighted by the compliment, batted her eyelashes playfully at the chef. "Oh, monsieur, where have you been hiding all this time? We can't have a man of such talent and charm sequestered in the kitchen!"

It was not until the shadows lengthened and the golden hues of afternoon faded into the dusky tones of early evening that Elizabeth and Harriet reluctantly parted ways.

"The morrow brings new tidings and perhaps fresh scandals to uncover," Harriet said as she gathered her things to take her leave. "Until next time, dear Lizzie."

As Elizabeth escorted Harriet to the door, bidding her a warm farewell, her gaze wandered beyond the confines of the manor. There, against the sprawling canvas of the heathland, a figure caught her eye—a silhouette that moved with purposeful strides under the encroaching veil of twilight. Beside him walked a woman, her chestnut hair catching the last rays of the sun, weaving threads of gold into the tapestry of the evening.

A frown creased Elizabeth's brow as recognition dawned, the playful light in her eyes dimming slightly. The woman was unmistakable—Molly Dawson. What business, Elizabeth wondered, could the manor's chef have with Molly, out there where the heath kissed the sky?

* * *

As the amber hues of the setting sun painted the sky, Henri and Molly made their way across the heathland, their steps in unison towards a place of quiet remembrance. Between them, they held a bundle of freshly picked wildflowers—a vibrant mosaic of red, yellow, and blue—each bloom a testament to life's fleeting beauty. The heath, with its sprawling expanse and the whisper of the wind, bore witness to their solemn journey.

Arriving at a nook of the earth, already graced with blooms from days past, they knelt, the evening's offering of flowers tenderly held between them. Tears, the silent heralds of Henri's sorrow, traced paths down his cheeks, causing Molly's heart to ache in its love for him.

"He would have been born soon, mon fils, if God was willing," Henri whispered, the pain and acceptance in his voice mingling with the hues of the dying light. Molly, moved by the depth of his emotion, clasped his hand tighter, a wordless vow of solidarity and shared sorrow.

Looking into Henri's eyes, Molly found the courage to voice her own path to closure. "I think...I think it's going to be alright," she whispered, her voice barely above the wind. "Our son...he was loved deeply...but I am finally ready to let him go. One day...we will meet him again. He is with the Father now."

Henri turned to face her, his gaze intense with a mix of loss and resolution. "He was my son, and he was taken. I've never had much in my life of my own I got to keep. But I am yours, and you are mine. Je suis à toi, and tu es à moi. And nothing is taking you from me," he vowed, the promise in his words as steadfast as the earth beneath them.

Together, they stood in silent vigil, the wildflowers laid to rest as the sun dipped below the horizon, its final rays casting long shadows across the heathland. The world around them faded into the background, leaving only the two of them, standing in the gathering darkness.

* * *

Now, as the final vestiges of daylight concede to the embrace of night, we turn our gaze back to the hallowed confines of the chapel, to observe how our esteemed Reverend Smythe has weathered the day. It's been an arduous day of diligent labor for our clergyman, not in sermon preparation nor in pastoral care, mind you, but in a task of equally divine importance: the meticulous inventory and quality assurance of the chapel's wine reserves.

Under the guise of this sacred duty, our dear Reverend has found himself partaking a bit too liberally in the sacramental bounty, embarking on a solitary voyage of vinous exploration that has seen him meander through the chapel in a state that might best be described as less than sober. The sacred space has borne witness to his spirited (in more ways than one) sojourn, as he, with the unsteady gait of a pilgrim tested by the spirit, knocked over candlesticks, sent scripture cascading in disarray, and offered up slurred homilies to an audience of shadows and echoes.

In the midst of his inebriated exploits, our Reverend Smythe found his imagination taking flight. As he wobbled precariously in the dimly lit chapel, his mind conjured up a most peculiar revision of biblical events.

"Imagine, if you will," he slurred to an audience of shadows, "Moses at the Red Sea, staff in hand, but lo, it is not water that parts before him, but the finest vintage, a divine merlot parting at his command!" The very thought sent him into a fit of giggles, the image of Israelites tip-toeing through rivers of red wine too delightful for his sodden brain to resist.

And then, with a hiccup that echoed through the hallowed hall, his mind danced to the tale of David and Goliath, where instead of a sling and stone, David bested the giant with a well-aimed bottle of sacred cabernet, the cork popping with divine precision to fell the behemoth. "Truly, the Lord's ways are mysterious and fermented," he mused, chuckling at the absurdity of his own reverie.

Not content with these embellishments, Reverend Smythe's imagination soared to the walls of Jericho, envisioning not the blast of trumpets, but a chorus of wine glasses, their clinks and clatters harmonizing to bring the city's defenses down in a cascade of celebratory bubbles. "And the walls came tumbling down," he sang, "under the assault of heavenly brut!"

In the apex of his drunken folly, he envisioned the Last Supper, where Jesus, in a moment of divine inspiration, turned not just water into wine, but the very stones of Jerusalem into aged oak barrels, each brimming with celestial vintages, a testament to the eternal banquet awaiting the faithful.

And thusly Reverend Smythe found himself sprawled inelegantly across a pew, his laughter mixing with snores in a discordant symphony. It was in this dubious repose that he fancied he heard the dulcet tones of an angelic visitor, beckoning him from his grape-induced reverie. Blinking into the dim light, he beheld a vision so resplendent, so ethereally beautiful, that he could scarce believe it anything but a celestial apparition.

"Reverend? Reverend Smythe? I hope I've not disturbed you," came the voice again, and with a clarity that gradually pierced the fog of his inebriation, Smythe recognized not an angel dispatched from the heavenly realms, but the earthly presence of Amelia Rutherford, her countenance concerned yet radiant in the chapel's muted glow.

"Miss Rutherford! My apologies," he slurred, a sheepish grin overtaking his features. "I was, ah, engaged in...ecclesiastical inventory. To what do I owe the pleasure of your visitation?"

Amelia stepped forward. "Reverend, I...I need to talk with you. It's important," she implored, her voice carrying the weight of untold troubles seeking solace and guidance.

"Ah, Miss Rutherford, I am honored," he mumbled, somehow managing to raise his chalice in a toast. "For in the vine, veritas—or was it in vino? No matter. Blessed are we, the seekers and the sippers alike!"

CHAPTER 5
MUTUAL FRIENDS

Beneath a vast blue sky, the ancient ruins of Whitby Abbey stand watch over the North Yorkshire coast, their weathered stones whispering tales of a past steeped in both piety and intrigue. Trailing a horse's length behind Amelia, Charles let the rhythmic cadence of hooves against the earth lull him into a state of reluctant reflection. "These stallions have displayed a modicum of quality," he mused with a measure of grudging acceptance. The venture of the morning, initiated at the cusp of dawn with the ambition of conquering the lofty vistas offered by Whitby, had transformed into an unexpected trial by fire for their mounts—a trial they had surprisingly surmounted, eliciting from him an admission of mild appreciation.

"Yet the token of my inheritance is both small and brief," he thought bitterly. "'Like a son to me,' Reginald said! Clearly the gap between 'son' and 'like a son' is wide where wills and inheritance are concerned. Still, the horses are something." Charles already had plans to meet that very evening with a local horse trader. The prospect of their sale, a mere drop in the ocean of his financial duress, brought forth a cascade of reflections upon his manifold ventures and misadventures in Manchester.

"'Investment', they said! 'The future of industry', they proclaimed!" he reminisced, with the vinegary aftertaste of hindsight. "Fortunes to be made, they told me!" Yet the cotton mills, once beheld as bastions of prosperity, had unraveled into fonts of fiscal ruin, their threads of promise tangled in the loom of market volatility. And then, the gambling dens—the less said about that, the better. "'A sure thing at the races', they assured! 'Bet on red', they declared!"

"Ah, the bitter draught of insolvency," he lamented. The planned sale of the stallions, though a matter of practical necessity, stung with the prick of concession, a tangible acknowledgment of his dwindling dominion over destiny.

Yet his gaze, roving as it was prone to do, found its anchor in Amelia. There she was, embodying a poise that starkly contrasted the rugged terrain beneath them—a living tribute to the countless days of their youth, when Ashford Manor's vast grounds served as their playground and classroom alike. Yet, it was the memory of another sojourn to Whitby Abbey that invaded his thoughts unbeckoned.

Reginald, in those days, had donned the mantle of the enlightened guide with an enthusiasm Charles could only describe as oppressively educational.

"Behold, the very stones where Abbess Hild convened her synod," Reginald had declared, gesturing grandly towards the ruins. "Imagine, if you will, the debates, the theological discourse..." Charles could almost still hear the drone of Reginald's voice as it had echoed off the ancient stones, a monologue as dry as the abbey's crumbled mortar. "'A veritable charm offensive,' they all declared of Reginald, a coded cipher for 'The man's wealth knows no bounds!'"

Reginald's tales had meandered from one historical event to the next with the tenacity of a hound on the scent. "Did you know," Reginald had said with a flourish, "that it was here, among these hallowed ruins, that the decision was made to calculate Easter using the method still employed today? Fascinating, is it not?" Fascinating, indeed, had been Charles' feigned reply, though Julian had been even less obliging: "I suppose that's some semblance of forward movement, but just imagine, a railway connecting Whitby directly to London! Progress, my dear Reginald, progress!"

Reginald, undaunted by Charles's simmering impatience or Julian's relentless march toward modernity, had continued to instruct on the historical beauty to anyone willing—or unwilling—to listen. "Observe the gothic elegance, the ethereal grace of lancet arches," he had enthused.

Charles smiled thinly at the memory. In the bloom of their adolescence, Charles and Amelia had stolen a moment of forbidden tenderness beneath those very arches.

But Reginald, ever vigilant, had, upon their return, issued a decree as stern as any edict. "Let there be a chasm between your affections," he had admonished. "And to think, not even a steed bequeathed for his surrogate daughter," Charles mused, a twinge of bitterness lacing his thoughts.

Amelia, the niece of Eleanor, and Charles, a cousin to Reginald, had been not merely guests but wards of Ashford Manor, brought under its expansive and shadow-draped eaves by the capricious hand of fate. It was within those venerable walls that Reginald, with a patriarch's ambition, sought to mould from their disparate sorrows a fraternal bond, to weave from tragedies a tapestry of siblinghood. Yet, despite his grand designs, the quiet corners and dimly lit passageways of the estate bore witness to an affection of a decidedly different nature.

Amelia's voice broke through Charles's musings, laced with light-hearted jest. "Are you moping again, Charles? Sometimes, I do believe your scowl is but a facet of your undeniable charm." Her words drew a reluctant smile.

Amelia's deep green eyes seemingly capturing the landscape around them. Around her neck hung a golden necklace, its red jewel catching the fading sunlight. "Shower your lady with gifts, they say," Charles reflected ruefully, trying to avoid thinking about what the necklace would have fetched on the market.

As they reached the cliffs' edge, the ocean unfolded before them, a limitless canvas of blue that stretched into eternity. Side by side, they paused, the ocean's roar a distant symphony to their shared silence.

"The necklace looks beautiful on you," Charles remarked softly, a trace of wistfulness in his tone. "Just, perhaps remove it before you're next around Eleanor."

Amelia smiled, the light of the setting sun reflecting in her eyes. "Should I be thanking you or our dear Lady Eleanor for my latest gift? But I doubt she'll miss it. She rarely does," she mused, her laughter mingling with the ocean's whisper. "I suppose I should be thankful that you deemed me worthy of this trinket...last time you overlooked me in favor of my young cousins and their governess."

Charles chuckled. "Elizabeth Blythe? You know she's too sanctimonious for me. Plus, she's always in Eleanor's shadow, so what chance would she have to ever flaunt my generous gifts?"

"Then it seems," Amelia rejoined, "you are doomed to lavish upon me all your ill-gotten treasures."

The ocean's vastness seemed to echo Amelia's next words. "The ocean is so freeing, don't you think? That's what I want for us. Not treasures...just a little house by the sea... you and me."

Charles began, "Amelia..." but she anticipated his thoughts, gently interrupting, "It doesn't have to be this way, you know? I don't think it's much of a secret who we are to each other. Reginald was the only one opposed, and, bless him, but he's no longer with us."

"Yes, someday, Amelia, someday," Charles acquiesced, a shadow of concern flitting across his face as his gaze lowered. "But...we have to be careful. And then there's the mess in Manchester I need to untangle myself from. If not, we might be looking for a house across the ocean," he joked.

"Don't let it wait long." Amelia's gaze also drifted downward, her hand instinctively resting on her belly.

By mid-afternoon, Charles and Amelia made their way back to the quaint guest cottage at the fringe of Ashford Manor estate, where Amelia resided temporarily. A fleeting moment of silence hovered as they stood at the doorstep, laden with an unspoken plea from Amelia, beseeching Charles to linger by her side.

Delicately, Charles revealed a small vial from the confines of his pocket, its glass shimmering with a verdant allure, encasing an amber liquid within. Catching Amelia's gaze, now clouded with a shimmer of apprehension, he softly urged, "Do remember, Amelia. Just a few drops, when you are ready, then allow yourself some rest. I expect this shall take some time and I will not be away long," his tone reassuring. "By nightfall, I shall be at your side once more."

A flicker of dismay danced across Amelia's features, her voice trembling slightly as she protested, "You mean to leave me now, at such an hour?" Her words hung between them, a gentle rebuke veiled in disbelief.

Charles, his countenance etched with resolve yet softened by affection, responded, "As I've told you, I must finalize the stallions' sale, but worry not, for I shan't tarry." His attempt to cloak his departure in necessity was met with a palpable tension.

"Promise me, Charles, that you will return to me this very night."

"Amelia, I promise. You won't even have time to miss me." And with a smile of farewell, Charles departed.

* * *

Reverend Smythe found himself in a most unenviable state. His head felt as if it were encased in a vice, each pulse a hammer upon the anvil of his skull. "What crown of thorns has been thrust upon my brow?" he lamented internally, immediately chiding himself for the blasphemy. "Forgive me, Father, for I know not what I do," he whispered into the emptiness of his quarters, his voice tinged with remorse and the faintest hint of mirth at his own melodrama.

Reverend Smythe reached with trembling hands for the bottle left perilously uncorked from the night prior. "Surely," he reasoned, "'My cup runneth over' speaks of a bountiful recovery." Thus, he poured himself a measure, not as a continuation of the previous night's folly but as a tentative step towards redemption, or so he told himself.

However, his solace was short-lived, for no sooner had he taken his first, tentative sip, savoring the false god's promise of relief, than a knock came at his door. At the first knock, he dismissed it as a figment of his troubled mind. The second knock found him wincing, hoping against hope for silence. But upon the third, he could no longer feign deafness. "Fine, then," he muttered under his breath, "I shall not follow Peter's path and deny thrice."

As he staggered towards the door, his mind spun a chaotic tapestry of thought. "The stray sheep indeed are both the shepherd's bane and blessing," he pondered, half-remembering some biblical parable or another. "Yet must I be haunted by spirits thrice in one night?" he lamented, oblivious to the sun's high stance in the sky.

Swinging the door wide, he was greeted by Harriet Westbrook. "I heard tell of your malaise, Reverend," she said, her voice laced with concern. "I've brought you some broth, and a bit of bread with butter, hoping it might ease your suffering." Her eyes, however, danced with the gleam of someone with an appetite for tidings far spicier than her soup.

Upon the sight of Harriet Westbrook bearing sustenance, Reverend Smythe's spirits lifted immeasurably. "Lo, 'tis said that 'Man shall not live by bread alone,' yet at this moment, bread—and broth—seem to be precisely what this man needs," he considered. Graciously, he ushered Miss Westbrook into his modest quarters, where she took a seat with the air of one settling in for an extended visit.

As the Reverend fervently engaged with the humble repast before him,

Harriet ventured, "You've had quite the burden of late, I'm sure, Reverend. Our little community is abuzz with the news of murder, of all things!"

"Indeed, Miss Westbrook," Smythe replied, his attention momentarily divided between acknowledging Harriet's observation and his ardent pursuit of nourishment. "These are trying times for us all."

Harriet, undeterred by the Reverend's divided focus, leaned in, her voice dropping to a hushed but urgent tone. "And to think, poison, of all methods! Our own little heathland turned scene of such clandestine darkness. I tell you, Reverend, if the police are to make any headway, they'll need all the divine intervention they can muster."

Internally, Harriet mused on the potential legacy of her investigative efforts. Her memoirs of the whole affair would make for quite the sensation. "'Death in the Dales'? No, too on the nose," she thought, though not without a certain fondness for the alliteration. "But the tale will need a telling, and who better than I to pen such a narrative?"

Continuing, she posed a question only half in jest. "I don't suppose anyone has felt compelled to confess their sins of a... *grave* nature to you?"

"No confessions of that gravity have graced my ears," Reverend Smythe responded with a shake of his head...and another sip from his cup.

Harriet was persistent. "Surely, Reverend, within your pastoral care, you've glimpsed stray sheep, or perhaps even wolves in sheep's clothing?"

Reverend Smythe, pausing to ladle a generous portion of broth into his mouth, savored the warmth that momentarily eased his woes before responding. "Indeed," he said, wiping his mouth with the back of his hand, "there may have been... certain revelations. But...," and here, the Reverend now tried dipping his bread, "..you will understand, this requires a level of discretion." His eyes wandered over to Harriet's plate of assorted breads and she passed over another.

Gratefully accepting the day's offering, the Reverend took a fortifying sip of wine, as if the liquid might steel him against the sobering self-awareness threatening to take hold regarding his own indiscretions. Harriet waited in anticipation as the Reverend continued, speaking between bites of bread soaked in broth. "It has come to my...hic...attention that Lord Reginald was perhaps about to be a father once more, outside the bonds of his marriage to Lady Eleanor."

Harriet could not hide her smile in excitement at this latest reveal. "A clandestine child! This adds a new layer, Reverend. Surely, we must inform the constabulary!"

The Reverend, with a sigh that sent crumbs flying, shook his head. "No, I believe this is an entirely separate matter." He paused, his contemplation interrupted by the involuntary vision of the Red Sea—red as the vintage in his goblet—cleaving in twain. He took another sip of wine, as if searching for the right words at the bottom of his cup. "Molly said—" he caught himself, realizing his blunder too late.

"Oh, Molly Dawson?" Harriet pounced on the name with the eagerness of a cat.

"Yes, well…," and here another baptizing of the bread in broth, "…the child was lost, apparently some months ago, and the affair, much like this bread,"— his hungry eyes gestured towards the half-eaten loaf—"remains largely unknown."

Harriet, undeterred by either the somber note to the tale or the Reverend's interest in finishing his meal, was already thinking ahead, her mind abuzz with the implications. The Reverend, observing her fervor, cautioned her between mouthfuls, "Prudence, Harriet. Stirring that pot will not win you any friends." He then happily realized he was stirring his own pot and brought another spoonful of broth to his lips.

Harriet nodded, for once slightly subdued. Excited as she was, even she felt restrained by the risks of spreading such a tale. "Reverend, perhaps other stories have been shared within these walls? One might even be persuaded to offer apple tart in exchange for such divine revelations," she teased, her voice lilting with humor as she eyed the nearly empty plate beside his elbow.

The Reverend paused, a piece of bread halfway to his mouth, as he regarded Harriet. "Well, there was a curious visit last night," he began, his brow furrowing as he attempted to sift through the fog of his memory. "Ah, yes, it was a silly matter really. Amelia seemed quite concerned over Charles and some girl," he recalled, the wine in his cup not aiding as much in his recollection as he had hoped.

Harriet's eyebrow arched, her interest clearly piqued. "Well, it's no secret those two are thick as thieves. But what girl?" she pressed.

The Reverend struggled to recall, his hand absentmindedly reaching for his wine glass again. "Rose? No, that's not right. Violet? No, not that either," he mumbled.

"Daisy?" Harriet suggested. "Lily?"

But the Reverend continued his mental search, oblivious to Harriet's growing list of floral names. Finally, a light of recognition flickered in his eyes. "Tansy! That was it. Tansy," he declared, with a look as self-satisfied as if he had discovered the holy grail itself.

Harriet looked up with a start. "Tansy? There's a girl named Tansy? What exactly did Amelia say?" Her voice carried a mixture of disbelief and excitement.

The Reverend again was struggling to remember, the details of the conversation as elusive as the location of Eden. "Well, Amelia was really in quite a state and not making much sense. But she said something like 'Charles was looking for Tansy' or 'Charles wants Tansy.' It was all a bit bizarre, and I confess I wondered if Amelia had been partaking a bit too much of the vine herself."

Harriet's cheeks were aglow with the thrill of the chase, her heart alight with visions of infamy and acclaim. She, Harriet Westbrook, had solved the Murder at the Moors. She hastily made her exit, leaving the Reverend to enjoy his heavenly manna while pondering whether that promised apple tart was—just perhaps—the forbidden fruit from the famed garden of Eden.

* * *

As they once again ascended the imposing steps to Ashford Manor, Constable Barkley, puffing slightly from the exertion, cast a dubious glance at his companion. "Oi, Inspector, what's the game plan then? Last time we was here, Lady Eleanor nearly had us tossed out on our earholes. What makes you think this time'll be any different, eh?"

Inspector Hargreaves offered Barkley a knowing smile, the corners of his mouth turning up in anticipation. "Ah, but Constable, our fortunes may well be in for a change. It has come to my attention through Julian that Lady Eleanor is currently away in York, busily entangled with the family barrister and estate affairs. Therefore, I deduced that now would be an opportune moment to engage in a bit of...shall we say, thorough inquiry with the remaining occupants. Methodically, of course."

"Well blow me down, Inspector! I didn't know you 'ad it in ya," Barkley said, his tone a mixture of surprise and admiration. "All this time, you've been preaching 'bout doing things 'by the book,' and 'ere you are, pulling a sly one like the best of 'em."

The Inspector's smile widened just a fraction. "Oh, rest assured, Constable, our approach shall remain strictly 'by the book.'"

But Barkley had questions. "Ere, what's that you're doing? Bangin' on your nose like that?"

Sighing, Inspector Hargreaves ceased tapping his finger to his nose. "Well, Constable, it may not be explicitly outlined within the pages of our procedural manuals, but there's certainly no rule against two dedicated officers of the law entering a domicile upon being granted entry, particularly if said entry is extended in the spirit of cooperation. And besides," he added, his voice lowering, "who's to say we won't uncover something...illuminating? Let's proceed, shall we?"

Freshly energized, Constable Barkley approached the grand door of Ashford Manor with a vigor that seemed to swell within him. He lifted his hand and delivered a series of knocks so vigorous and protracted that they could have awakened the slumbering echoes of the moor itself.

Scarcely had the last echo of his authoritative rapping faded when a cacophony of screams and the distinct sound of porcelain shattering against the unforgiving floors of the manor filled the air. Barkley and Hargreaves exchanged a look, their eyebrows arching in unison.

The door swung open to reveal Thomas Graves standing as pristine and unbothered as if the manor were enveloped in the most serene silence rather than echoing with chaotic disarray. "Good afternoon, Inspector Hargreaves, Constable Barkley," he greeted, his voice steady and calm.

Constable Barkley blurted out, "Oi! What in the blazes is happening in there?

Sounds like bloody murder!"

"That would be the chef," Graves replied coolly, even as another symphony of crashes and yells filled the air. "It appears there was a... mishap in the kitchen."

"It just sounds like a lot of crazed yelling to me, nothing like I ever heard!" Barkley exclaimed, trying to peer past Graves into the source of the commotion. "Why so much yelling in the kitchen, eh? Always causing this much ruckus to bake some bread?"

The butler allowed one eyebrow to arch ever so slightly as he replied, "I'm afraid he considers himself something of an artist, sir."

Inspector Hargreaves seized the opportunity presented by the cacophony emanating from the kitchen. "It appears, Mr. Graves, that we might benefit from a brief colloquy with your chef before our departure. No stone unturned, every possibility meticulously accounted for, you understand. In addition, the Constable and I find ourselves with a handful of inquiries for the household's denizens. In the interest of thoroughness, I trust we might be afforded entry?"

Thomas Graves regarded the two lawmen with a measured gaze. After a moment's consideration, he conceded, "Yes, of course. Please," and stepped aside to grant them access.

Crossing the threshold, Constable Barkley's voice took on the edge of a man not just walking into a manor but into the fray. "You ain't gonna get all shy on us now, are ya? Got a hunch you're sat on a pile of juicy titbits that could help us out, ain't ya? I reckon nothing dodgy goes down in this gaff without it catching your eye, right?" His gaze drilled into Graves, his eyes narrowing.

Thomas Graves met the Constable's challenge smoothly. "I endeavor to remain informed of all matters pertinent to ensuring the seamless daily functioning of Ashford Manor," he responded.

Barkley amped up the pressure. "And keeping this ship sailing smooth don't cover keeping the lordship from popping his clogs too soon, does it? Come on then, spill it—who was the last to clap eyes on him breathing?" The Constable's eyes narrowed further still.

Graves began, "I can't say for sure, sir," maintaining his unruffled stance. "I had the honour of serving him his afternoon brew in the drawing room. 'Twas Lady Eleanor who later stumbled upon him in his study, departed from this world."

At this, Constable Barkley's eyes squinted with all the intensity of an East

End barrow boy suspecting he's been short-changed, his gaze burrowing deeper until, abruptly, he realized his eyelids had conspired to leave him in darkness. With a start, he snapped them open, a muddle of confusion and resolve playing across his features.

A brisk knock suddenly sliced through the thick tension swaddling the trio in the entry foyer like a knife through butter. Mr. Graves, in a move now as familiar as the morning's first cup of tea, swung the manor's grand door wide, only to find Harriet Westbrook quivering on the doorstep, ablaze with the sort of news that could set the Thames alight.

Before Graves could respond to her inquiry regarding Lizzie, Harriet's eyes darted to the lawmen, her excitement only escalating like a runaway carriage at the sight of them. "Oh! Inspector and Constable!!" she burst out. "Fortune smiles upon us! I've not only cracked your case but practically blown it to smithereens!"

Graves, along with Inspector Hargreaves and Constable Barkley, could only stare in a mix of confusion and bewilderment. Harriet pressed on, her voice tinged with triumph. "I have it on the most solid of authorities—practically the Gospel truth—that Charles Windham is your culprit. A stern chat with him, if you would be so kind, gentlemen, and you shall unearth his dastardly deeds with the tansy poison you've been chasing, no doubt about it!"

Inspector Hargreaves, momentarily adrift in the sea of Harriet's enthusiasm, recognized the potential lead before him and righted his ship with the skill of a seasoned sailor. Turning on his heel to face Mr. Graves, his tone was urgent, "Mr. Graves, any sightings of Charles Windham today?"

Graves, for once quite taken aback resembled a startled owl caught in the lantern light. Still, he quickly regained his composure, though a hint of disbelief lingered in his voice. "Indeed, he is currently on the estate. Mr. Charles mentioned he'd be at the stables, preparing for a business engagement slated within the hour."

Inspector Hargreaves turned to Constable Barkley. With a sly tap of his nose, he remarked, "See? The mystery's unraveling right before our eyes. 'By the book.'"

At that, Harriet's excitement surged anew. "Oh, yes! You absolutely must buy my book once I'm finished," she exclaimed, nearly vibrating with anticipation. "'The Poisoned Patriarch'? Or perhaps 'Killing Cousin'?"

The Inspector and Constable exchanged a glance then stared back at Harriet Westbrook, who still stood standing on the doorstep. Inspector Hargreaves finally responded, "Yes, well, thank you for your...er, enthusiastic assistance in this matter. Rest assured, we'll take it from here and consult you should we require further...insight."

Leaning closer to Hargreaves, Constable Barkley's voice dropped to a whisper. "Sir, ain't Charles the wrong 'un for this? Weren't we after evidence pointin' to Lady Eleanor being the one what done it?"

Hargreaves, his expression solemn, replied, "I'm afraid Julian Ashford will have to accept his progress as it chooses to unfold. As I always say, we're conducting this investigation by the book, and I, for one, am keen to conclude this particular book posthaste. Now, let us go have that stern chat with Charles Windham and bring this sorry chapter to a close."

CHAPTER 6
HARD TIMES

Ashford Manor, looming like a brooding gargoyle perched ominously upon the North York Moors, casts its foreboding shadow beneath a sky set aflame by the waning embers of day. Within, Mr. Graves, the silent ferryman, guides Inspector Hargreaves and Constable Barkley through its veined corridors, air rich with the legacy of beeswax and the whispered tales of timeworn oak. The Ashfords, captured in oils, survey their domain with a vigilance that transcends mortality, their visages a gallery of judgment upon the interlopers.

The portrait of Lord Edward Ashford presides over this realm not through noble sacrifice but upon the bent backs and broken spirits of those consigned to toil without respite or recognition. "Ensure the silver gleams, Martha. Lord Ashford prefers to see his reflection in every piece," one can almost hear Lord Edward's stern command echoing through the centuries, his icy blue eyes scrutinizing a maid as she scurries past with her cleaning cloth.

Nearby, Lady Margery's portrait, ensconced in her frame like a queen upon her throne, appears to survey the grand hall with an air of detached amusement. "Mind the cobwebs in the upper corners, won't you? We wouldn't want to give the impression we entertain spiders as guests," her eyes twinkle with a mischief that belies her otherwise stoic demeanor.

As Hargreaves and Barkley wander deeper into the heart of this ancient edifice, they find themselves under the piercing blue eyes of the Ashford lords and ladies who came before, each seeming to observe, to judge, the manifold secrets and sins that unfold within these walls. In life, the elite of Ashford Manor scarcely spared a glance for those who served them; in death, their painted eyes betray a curious, ceaseless vigilance—a silent testament to the countless secrets witnessed but never shared.

Finally emerging from the manor, the three men step into the cool embrace of the evening air. Mr. Graves, with a solemn gesture, directs Inspector Hargreaves and Constable Barkley toward the stables. Once out of earshot of Mr. Graves, Inspector Hargreaves breaks the silence, his voice slicing through the dense air with the ease of a well-used blade. "So, Constable, are you primed for that stern chat with Mr. Windham?" he began. "I'm of the belief we've netted our fish, but the task will be considerably smoother should we coax a confession from his own lips."

The Inspector continued. "You see, one of us adopts a rather... zealously threatening posture towards our Mr. Windham. Thus allowing the other the golden opportunity to emerge as the man's newfound 'friend'. A touch of the carrot and the stick together, if you will."

Constable Barkley, his brows knitting in confusion, struggled momentarily with the concept. "But sir," he interjected, "how's that gonna work, then? I mean, if we're both standing there, and he knows we're both coppers, how's he to believe one of us is his mate all of a sudden?"

The Inspector, unfazed by the Constable's skepticism, clapped him on the back with a collegial laugh and allowed himself yet another sly tap on the nose.

As they continued their trek towards the stables, the path underfoot became a mottled tapestry of darkness and light, the outlines of trees whipping back and forth in the wind. Barkley, scratching his head in a moment of deep thought, bombarded the Inspector with a barrage of questions. "Oi, do I start hollerin' at him from the off, or is it more like a slow boil, yeah?" he began. Then, with a frown that creased his forehead, he ventured further into the strategy's nuances. "Suppose he asks for a glass of water, mid-interrogation-like. Do I bark at 'im to lap it up from the floor, or do I hand it over nice and gentle, like a peace offering?" His eyes suddenly narrowed. "But 'ang on a tick, if you're playin' his mate and I'm the brute, don't that make me the odd one out?"

As they made their final approach to the stables, the Inspector and Constable found Charles Windham, who managed an air of disaffected impatience as he awaited the arrival of the horse trader. Constable Barkley, stepping forward with a determination born of their recent strategizing, launched into their carefully laid plan. "Halt, you!" he barked, adopting a stance that he hoped conveyed authority and suspicion. Charles—who was engaged in no activity whatsoever that he could "halt" looked around in an attempt to decipher a hidden explanation for the Constable's outburst. Barkley pressed his charge. "What might be the reason you're lingering around the stables, eh? Per'aps planning to make a sneaky getaway on one of these horses, are we?"

Charles regarded the Constable with a mix of disbelief and amusement. After a moment's pause, where he seemed to debate the wisdom of a sharp retort, a smirk played across his lips. "You're too late to prevent my grand escape, gentlemen," he quipped, leaning against the stable door with feigned nonchalance. "I'm only now returning after a day's ride. Seems you'll have to find another villain to chase."

Inspector Hargreaves favored Mr. Windham with a smile that strained at the edges. "Do excuse the Constable, would you? His enthusiasm occasionally overshadows his reason. Quite the bulldog when he latches onto something," he explained, his grin bordering on the grotesque.

"And what of this horse trader—merely a figment of your elaborate schemes, or an actual accomplice in your misdeeds?" Barkley boomed.

Charles raised an eyebrow. "Ah, yes, my notorious horse trading ring. You've caught me red-handed. Do proceed with the handcuffs, or is there a manual you must consult first for such occasions?"

The Inspector turned to Barkley with a frown that bordered on genuine irritation. "Constable, must you always lead with such aggression? You're agitating our... friend here," he chastised, his tone dripping with condescension.

Barkley leaned in closer to Hargreaves. "And perhaps, Inspector, if you showed a bit more backbone instead of flappin' your gums like a market fishwife, we'd have this scoundrel shaking in his boots by now!"

The Inspector, his patience fraying like an old rope, countered with a steely calm that belied his irritation. "And perhaps, Constable, if you used your head for something other than a hat rack, we'd progress beyond schoolyard tactics and actually glean something useful from Mr. Windham here."

Suddenly, Barkley whirled back to Charles, his eyes alight with a revelation as sudden as it was unfounded. "Aha! The truth unveils itself!" he exclaimed dramatically. "Conspiring to turn our own machinations against us whilst you recline in amusement!"

Charles parried with ease. "Truly, Constable, my plots are far less Byzantine than yours. I merely savor the evening's theatrics," he said.

Barkley pressed on. "In quite a hurry to liquidate your inheritance, I observe. A dire need for coin, perhaps? Lord Reginald's untimely demise most convenient for your purposes!"

Adopting an affability that could smother a fire, Inspector Hargreaves placed an arm around Charles, guiding him a few paces away from the agitated

Constable. "I really must apologize for Barkley. He's been itching to prove himself, a tad overeager, you know," the Inspector said, his tone soothing yet patronizing. "But you should be thankful he's not in the same mood as when we caught a simple thief not two weeks ago. Awful bloody business, that was. Imagine if he was really riled up! Now, what would be best, I think, is if you just answer a few of our questions. It'll put the Constable's mind at ease. You have no objection to joining us for a bit of questioning at our office, do you? We've set up an office not far from here for the time being."

Charles's thoughts raced to Amelia, and his retort was sharp and swift. "An urgent engagement awaits me," his voice tinged with frustration as he glanced momentarily at his pocket watch. "I'm sure gentlemen of your distinction can appreciate the importance of timely obligations."

Inspector Hargreaves tightened his grip slightly on Charles's shoulder, steering him away from Barkley's looming figure. "Absolutely, Mr. Windham, and while we understand your schedule, surely your horse trade can await another day while we clear up more pressing matters," he said soothingly. "It's all standard procedure, you see. Regulations and such. We simply must do things by the book."

"Oi, just a minute!" Barkley interjected, his suspicion clear. "Don't think we're just going to chat here and let you off easy. So, what is it then, you've got something to hide, eh?" His voice boomed across the stable yard, adding a palpable threat to his words.

Charles' thoughts raced, but, outwardly, he sought to maintain a veneer of composure. "Gentlemen, I assure you, whatever questions you have, I can answer just as well here as anywhere else. There's no need for offices or formalities."

Inspector Hargreaves chuckled lightly, attempting to smooth over the tension. "Mr. Windham, I fear the Constable's fervor may be a bit unsettling, but we really must insist on a more... appropriate setting for these discussions. It's merely following protocol, ensuring all is in order."

Barkley, stepping closer, narrowed his eyes. "A simple man with nothing to hide wouldn't shy away from a formal inquiry unless, of course, there's more to the story. You're not avoiding a little trip to our office, are you?"

At this, Charles's facade momentarily faltered, revealing a flicker of genuine disquiet swiftly overrun by indignation. "Insolence! For such baseless slander, I could see you stripped of your badge, Constable!"

Hargreaves' friendly grip on Charles' shoulder became firmer still so that Charles even winced under the pressure, though the Inspector kept his unsettling smile firmly on. "Consider this, Mr. Windham: a quick visit to our office, a brief chat to clarify these matters, and you'll be free to meet your engagements with no shadow of suspicion."

"Very well, gentlemen," Charles sighed, his voice laced with resignation, "lead the way."

The trio set off towards the waiting carriage, their path lit by the flaming embers of the setting sun. The walk was a silent procession, punctuated only by the gravel crunching under their boots and the occasional hoot of a distant owl.

Arriving at the carriage the trio tried to fit themselves within the confined space. The Constable, with his robust frame, took up more than his fair share, pushing Charles and the Inspector uncomfortably close. "Bit of a squeeze, eh?" the Inspector chuckled, trying to lighten the mood, though the close quarters only served to heighten Charles's sense of detainment.

As the carriage creaked into motion, it trundled through the breathtaking scenery of the North York Moors. The vast, open landscapes whizzed by, a stark contrast to the cramped, tense atmosphere inside the carriage. "We're using a new office at Goathland Station," the Inspector explained, his voice barely rising above the rattle of the wheels. "It's for the Administration of Railways and Societal Advancement. Not officially opened yet, but Julian Ashford was kind enough to let us use the space for our investigations."

Charles listened, but without paying attention. Eventually, the carriage pulled up to Goathland Station, its quaint charm dimly lit by the station lamps. Charles and Constable Barkley disembarked, with Charles feeling every bit the captive as he was led towards the yet-to-be-used office.

Hargreaves turned to his colleague as Barkley stepped onto the platform, his voice low. "Constable, why don't you go ahead and make Mr. Windham comfortable in our new accommodations and start with the questions? I need to make a quick check-in on our friend," he said, his eyes darting slightly as he spoke.

Barkley's brow furrowed deeper, a visible sign of his bewilderment. "Our friend, sir?" he queried.

The Inspector, a trace of exasperation seeping into his demeanor, began an elaborate series of pantomimes. He started with slicing motions through the air, each pass growing more exaggerated. As Barkley watched with increasing perplexity, the Inspector's gestures escalated into a dramatic performance.

"Is that a chef baking a cake?" Barkley guessed, squinting at the Inspector's flailing arms. "This isn't about a birthday surprise, is it?"

Exasperated beyond measure, the Inspector halted his performance, stood straight, and pointed emphatically towards his chest, mimicking an incision with a stern look.

"Ahh, right!" Barkley exclaimed, his face suddenly lighting up with understanding. "Our completely nondescript and entirely unmedical friend!" Barkley offered, winking conspiratorially as he turned to lead Charles towards the office and down the dimly lit platform of Goathland Station, the evening mist swirling around them. The station lay silent and somber under the watchful gaze of the moon, its pale light casting long shadows across the empty platform.

Their footsteps echoing ominously in the quiet night. The air was thick with the scent of damp moss and the distant aroma of burning coal from the last train's departure. They approached a solitary door at the far end of the platform, marked by a freshly painted sign: "Administration of Railways and Societal Advancement." The door creaked open into a stark, uninviting space, still smelling of new paint and sawdust—an office yet to be christened by the daily grind of bureaucracy.

Inside, the office was sparsely furnished with a sturdy wooden desk, a couple of hard-backed chairs, and a lone gas lamp flickering hesitantly in the drafty room. The walls, bare except for a few framed railway maps, echoed back their every movement, amplifying the sense of isolation.

Without warning, Barkley's demeanor shifted as they entered the stark office. He grabbed a set of clunky iron handcuffs from the desk drawer. With a swift movement born of many such prior applications, he clamped them around Charles's wrists, the metal biting coldly into his flesh.

"Alright, cut the charade," Barkley growled. "I already know what you did. We know about the poison. Give me an honest answer, or you'll wish to God you had," he threatened, his face inches from Charles's, eyes burning with a fierce certainty.

Charles winced at the sudden tightness of the handcuffs, his mind racing in confusion and panic. *Poison? They think I poisoned Reginald?* His heart hammered against his ribcage.

The flickering light from the gas lamp cast eerie shadows across Barkley's determined face, turning his features into something grotesque and menacing. As Barkley loomed over him, the stark reality of his perilous position struck Charles with chilling clarity. Barkley's stance hardened as he leaned in closer, his voice low and menacing. "Oh, I have ways of getting to the truth," he whispered, his eyes gleaming with menace in the flickering gaslight. Attempting to mimic the Inspector's earlier finesse, he tapped a fat finger against his nose. "And everything by the book, of course," he added, with a smirk that twisted his lips.

Charles, his wrists chafing under the handcuffs, struggled to keep his voice calm. "I swear to you, I haven't poisoned anyone. I don't know what you're talking about!" he protested, his voice cracking under the strain.

As they spoke, the whistle of an arriving train pierced the night, its mournful cry slicing through the tense atmosphere of the office. The walls vibrated faintly as the train rolled into the station, the sound of its heavy wheels grinding against the tracks filled the room with a resonant thunder. The office seemed to shudder, as if it too, felt the gravity of Charles's plight.

The train came to a halting screech, its brakes shrieking in the still night, echoing off the bare walls and amplifying the sense of impending doom. Barkley, undeterred by the cacophony, leaned forward, his face mere inches from Charles's. "Don't play the fool with me, Windham. If you think this noise can cover your lies, you're sorely mistaken." After a pause, he added. "Might drown out some screams though."

Charles, each word a plea, continued to assert his innocence amidst the clamor. "Please, you have to listen to me. I didn't even know about any poison—"

His words were abruptly drowned out by the renewed roar as the train departed from the station, the office trembling with the force of the locomotive's power. Barkley, his expression unyielding, watched Charles's every reaction, the shadows thrown by the gas lamp making his features appear even more malevolent. As the last of the train's noise faded into the distance, leaving behind a haunting silence, he straightened up, fixing Charles with a steely gaze.

"Last stop, Windham," Barkley intoned ominously, his eyes narrowing into slits of suspicion. "Now or never."

As Barkley leaned in, his breath cold and menacing against Charles's face, he taunted, "Got your hands on some tans-eh, did you? Nice way of making it look natural, was it?"

The full weight of Barkley's implication crashed down upon Charles. *They think the tansy was for Reginald!* As the absurdity of the accusation struck him, a wild, disquieting laughter burst from him. The sound was sharp and unnerving, echoing against the stark office walls, filling the room with its manic energy.

"This is madness," Charles gasped, his voice a blend of hysteria and disbelief.

Barkley recoiled slightly, his brow furrowing deeper as he assessed Charles with renewed wariness. The laugh, chilling and seemingly without end, seemed to confirm the darkness Barkley suspected lay behind Charles's genteel facade. "What's so funny, eh?" Barkley snapped, his tone hardening. "You find poisoning folk a laughing matter now, do you?"

As the reality of his situation sank in, Charles's thoughts involuntarily flickered to Amelia. *'Promise me,' she said!* The memory of her pleading echoed in his mind. He worried about the lateness of the hour, her being alone, each passing moment stretching into an eternity of dread.

Increasingly desperate, Charles's resolve began to crack under Barkley's relentless interrogation. "You bloody fool! The tansy was not for Reginald! It was for—" He caught himself, clamping his mouth shut as if the words

74

themselves were traitorous.

Barkley's eyes narrowed, his suspicion morphing into a mix of intrigue and accusation. "So you're telling me it wasn't Reginald you killed with the tans-eh, it was some other bloke? How many murders do I have to solve for this blasted family?!" he demanded, his tone laced with frustration and ever growing impatience.

Charles shook his head vigorously, "No, no, you don't understand," he muttered, the chains of the handcuffs clinking ominously. "It was to help a woman with child," he muttered quietly at last.

As Barkley continued his questioning, he applied pressure—not enough to cause lasting harm but enough to emphasize his words with a grim physicality. "Out with it then! Who was the woman, eh? And what of the child, hmm?"

Charles trembled, the weight of his decisions pressing down on him. He thought of Amelia, her image a beacon in the growing darkness of his predicament, as he clung to his last shred of loyalty. His eyes darted around the room as if seeking an escape that words would not offer.

Barkley's voice cut through the tense silence that had settled in the stark office. "So that's the way it's gonna be, is it? For once, nothing to say for yourself?" He leaned back against the sparse desk, arms folded, eyes locked on Charles. "Well, that's alright. You see, the Inspector is having his own little chat at the moment. Let's see what he says on his return, about whether Reginald had a dose of that tansy to help him off to that final sleep."

The room seemed to contract around Charles, the walls inching closer with each word Barkley spat. The flickering gas lamp cast ghostly shadows, dancing like specters across the cold walls, mirroring the chill that had settled deep in Charles's bones.

* * *

As Inspector Hargreaves's carriage trundled across the expanse of the moorland, his mind indulged in the self-congratulatory revelry of his own strategic prowess. Nestled within the creaking confines of well-worn leather, he regarded himself with a smug satisfaction seldom seen but in the mirror of one's own vanity.

"Ah, Constable Barkley," he mused, his chuckle harmonizing with the rhythmic clopping of hooves, "as green as the spring yet unseasoned by the sun. A veritable sapling flailing in the gales of justice." The Inspector's amusement at his metaphor was evident in the slight curl of his lip. "There he is, out there, playing the heavy—blundering about like a bull in a china shop. Good fortune to him, though the odds of extracting a confession from Charles Windham are as likely as blood from a stone."

The carriage's path wound through the heathery sea, a silhouette against the canvas of the evening stars. Hargreaves's mind danced from one thought to the next. "Charles Windham, cousin to our dear departed Lord Reginald, nearly a son in all but blood. To accuse him so boldly? A delicious scandal, indeed, yet such delectable morsels must be savored from a distance, served cold to those with an appetite for spectacle."

Reclining further into the embrace of his leathery throne, the Inspector envisioned the grand chessboard of his profession. "Let young Barkley relish the fleeting warmth of potential glory. Meanwhile, I shall ply the more subtle streams," he plotted with a grin that spread like a shadow at dusk. "A suspect on one hand, a scapegoat on the other—Barkley, if need be. It's a checkmate either way. Should the tempest unleash its fury, it shall find me on terra firma, well away from its wrath."

His thoughts meandered to the lofty peaks of career advancement—a landscape he navigated with the skill of a seasoned cartographer. "Promotions are bestowed upon those who deliver, indeed, but also upon those who dodge the deluge." He contemplated his next maneuvers, his mind deftly sorting through the possibilities like a gambler shuffling his cards. "If the ship must rock, let Barkley be the one to shake the sails. And may heaven help him!"

"It is I who will return with the definitive medical evidence," he thought, anticipation tingling through him as he considered his upcoming visit to Dr. Fletcher. The thought of tansy detected in the autopsy samples was electrifying. "Should tansy be found, the murder is as good as solved. Each piece will fall into place, a testimony to my orchestration."

And yet, a shadow of doubt crept in, the slight furrow of his brow betraying his usual composure. "And if not, well, better to be in my shoes than Barkley's, who may well find himself dangling precariously from a limb with nary a branch to break his fall."

Adjusting his cufflinks—a gesture as meticulous as his planning—Hargreaves prepared for the evening that might well dictate the trajectory of the investigation and, more importantly, the course of his own career.

The carriage creaked to a halt before Dr. Fletcher's residence, its silhouette revealing itself through the swirling mist. The last ghosts of daylight draped the scene in an expectant hush, the night air thick with the tension of awaited revelations. Hargreaves stepped out, the gravel crunching underfoot as he approached the heavy wooden door of the residence. His knock echoed, a solid, foreboding sound that seemed to hang in the air. Moments later, a voice boomed from within, startlingly loud in the quiet evening.

"Announce yourself!" Dr. Fletcher's voice rang out as if he were commanding a regiment rather than greeting a visitor.

"It's Inspector Hargreaves, Doctor. I come in peace," Hargreaves replied with a chuckle.

The door swung wide to reveal Dr. Fletcher, a figure as imposing as his booming voice. "Ah, the esteemed Inspector! Enter, enter!" he exclaimed with a theatrical flourish, his broad grin beckoning Hargreaves into the shadowy foyer.

Stepping into the dimly lit hall, Hargreaves found himself amidst a veritable cabinet of curiosities. The walls and shelves brimmed with artifacts of Dr. Fletcher's eclectic passions. A military saber and an ornately carved blunderbuss were displayed on a shelf across the room. Disturbingly close at hand, a collection of preserved creatures floated in glass jars, each suspended in a formaldehyde ballet—frogs with extra limbs, a two-headed snake, and what appeared to be the desiccated remains of a bat with an unusually human-like face. Above the fireplace, a dusty globe neighbored a pair of dueling pistols, while scientific tools—a brass microscope, an electrostatic machine, and an intriguingly labeled 'Etheric Force Detector'—lay scattered about, each whispering tales of esoteric adventures.

"Can I tempt you with a robust tipple, Inspector?" Dr. Fletcher inquired, moving toward a grand cabinet filled with spirits. With a showman's gesture, he produced a bottle of Absinthe, the 'Green Fairy', its label faded like a forgotten secret.

"Nothing stirs the mind quite like the Fairy," chuckled Dr. Fletcher, preparing the absinthe with a ritualistic precision. He placed a slotted spoon over the glass, balanced a sugar cube atop, and drizzled ice-cold water until the liquid bloomed into a cloudy, opalescent green.

"Behold, a concoction as enigmatic and potent as the mysteries we unravel," declared Dr. Fletcher, presenting the glass to Hargreaves.

The strong, anise-flavored liquor was both a shock and a delight, its herbal complexity unfolding with each sip, much like the layers of the case Hargreaves was entangled in. Surrounded by the bizarre and the grotesque, with a glass of absinthe in hand, he felt momentarily as if he had stepped into another world.

"I've come to check on the progress of your studies, Doctor. The samples from the autopsy of Lord Reginald," Hargreaves broached the subject as he took a sip.

Dr. Fletcher's eyes lit up, a spark of enthusiasm igniting within. "Ah, the marvels of science! Did you know, from those very samples, I deduced Lord Reginald's proclivity for exotic tobaccos? And his liver, well, that told tales of many a spirited night!" he began, his voice booming with excitement. "Moreover, his heart—ah, his heart was a weak vessel, strained beyond its humble capacities. It seems the poor organ was quite spent, much like the faded springs of an old clock."

As Dr. Fletcher prattled on, detailing each finding with the gusto of a conductor leading an orchestra, Hargreaves' attention began to drift. The absinthe tingled on his tongue, its effects subtly altering his perception. The shadows in the room seemed to stretch and twist, the scientific oddities around him coming eerily to life in his increasingly blurred vision.

Hargreaves remained keen to steer the conversation back to the matter at hand, despite the growing oddities around him. "Fascinating, truly, Doctor," he said, ducking reflexively as a taxidermized bat, previously motionless, seemed to flap its leathery wings overhead, casting eerie, fluttering shadows against the dim walls. "But about the poisons—foxglove, perhaps? Or maybe... tansy?" he inquired, his voice tinged with hopeful urgency, even as the room appeared to sway gently around him, the walls pulsating as if breathing. The room seemed to pulse with a life of its own, the bottled creatures appearing to squirm in their jars. The military relics, hung proudly on the walls, clanged and echoed phantom battles of yore, their sounds merging with Fletcher's booming declarations.

Dr. Fletcher paused, standing amidst his collection of macabre and bizarre artifacts, which seemed to Hargreaves to be inching closer, their shadows dancing menacingly in the flickering lamp light. The doctor began to pace, his voice booming as if addressing a battalion. "Ah, Inspector, in the realm of science, we are but humble soldiers marching through a fog of data! We deal with possibilities and probabilities! In my reconnaissance mission through the biological terrain of our dear departed lord, could these named enemies be present? Yes, perhaps. But perhaps not," he declared, his voice echoing off the walls, becoming part of the cacophony of noises filling the room.

As the effects of the absinthe deepened, Hargreaves' vision began to fragment. Multiple Dr. Fletchers appeared before him, each one a specter clad in a lab coat, waving arms theatrically. They marched around him in a surreal parade, shouting about the probabilities and possibilities, their voices overlapping in a dissonant chorus. "A realm of uncertainties, Inspector! A battlefield where our foes might be shadows!" they cried, their figures multiplying and then converging. Caught in this tempest, Hargreaves felt as if he were standing in the midst of a surreal battle, with scientific soldiers clamoring around him, each iteration of Fletcher more animated and dramatic than the last.

"I see," Hargreaves murmured, his frustration mounting as he addressed the room filled with multiple flickering images of Dr. Fletcher, hoping his question would reach the real one. "Can you not simply tell me if Lord Reginald was killed with tansy? Just a straight answer, Doctor!"

The apparitions of Dr. Fletcher around the room each began to respond, their voices a chorus of scientific caution. "Inspector, you must understand, science does not bow to the simplicity of yes or no answers. We navigate through probabilities and evidence," they intoned in unison, their spectral forms wavering like a mirage.

Cutting through the cacophony, the hopefully real Dr. Fletcher stepped forward, his presence momentarily grounding in its certainty. "The odds, as I have assessed them through rigorous examination, do not exceed two or three out of ten. It is not definitive, Inspector," he stated clearly, his voice a single thread of reason amidst the tumult.

This clarification, though sobering, sank into Hargreaves like a stone into a deep lake, the ripples of disappointment spreading through his thoughts. The potential clarity he had hoped for was now thoroughly dissolved into the misty ambiguity of scientific investigation. The room's oddities swirled around him in a dizzying dance, echoing the chaos of his thoughts.

Reluctantly accepting the elusive nature of the evidence, Hargreaves steadied himself against a table, taking a moment to gather his wits. "Thank you, Doctor," he said with strained civility, his voice cutting through the lingering echoes of Fletcher's bombastic explanations as he headed for the exit.

Stepping forth into the crisp embrace of the evening air, Inspector Hargreaves inhaled deeply, seeking to dispel the fantastical visions that had so vividly danced before his eyes within the confines of Dr. Fletcher's eccentric sanctuary. He strode towards his carriage, his footsteps echoing against the stone path, a lonely sound in the stillness of the night. As he reached for the carriage door, a jolt of surprise arrested his movement—Constable Barkley was already ensconced within, his form an eerie silhouette bathed in the ghostly luminescence of the moon.

"Well, he is along for the ride now," Hargreaves mused quietly as he climbed into the carriage beside the spectral Constable. "When the storm comes, it finds Barkley at the helm, not me." This thought, cold as the night air, brought him a grim comfort.

As the carriage rattled away from the doctor's abode, the moorland landscape swept by under a wash of ethereal moonlight. Barkley, or his apparitional semblance, turned toward Hargreaves, his features etched with a spectral concern. "Oi, guv'nor, reckon we might've been a bit overzealous with that Windham fellow, eh?" his voice floated in the confined space, tinged with regret.

Hargreaves, his laughter echoing hollowly against the carriage walls, replied, "You played the bad copper with aplomb, Barkley," his words dripping with a sardonic mirth.

Suddenly, a wail tore through the tranquility of the night, a mournful cry that seemed to emanate from the depths of the moor itself. Hargreaves' gaze snapped to the window, where the sight of a train slicing across the distant landscape brought a momentary reprieve—just a mechanical specter, not a ghostly one. Yet, as he turned back, his breath hitched. There, across from him, sat the spectral figure of Lord Reginald Ashford, his icy blue gaze piercing the shadows of the carriage.

Barkley squinted towards the apparition. "That there Reginald, he a real specter, or just another one of them hallucinations, like meself?" he queried.

Lord Reginald's ghost, ethereal yet imposing, addressed Hargreaves with a chill that matched the moorland frost. "Are you the best my fool brother could muster? Is there none finer to seek justice for my untimely demise?" His words, heavy with an otherworldly accusation, lingered malignantly in the air.

"Close your eyes, Inspector," Barkley suggested, his tone half jest, half desperate. "If we can't see him, surely he can't haunt us, right?"

With a resigned sigh, Hargreaves nodded. "Very well, on three. One, two, three—" Together, they shut their eyes, the carriage plunging into a silence punctuated only by the rhythmic clatter of wheels and their tense breathing. Yet it seemed to Hargreaves that the spectral presence of Lord Reginald persisted, his disdain palpable as he surveyed the denying duo. Though, after a lingering moment, the apparition accepted their stubborn refusal to acknowledge him, fading slowly into the night and away from Hargreaves' troubled mind, leaving behind only the chill of his parting words and the dark silhouette of the moorland slipping by.

* * *

Elizabeth Blythe was halfway through instructing Emma and Jenny on the finer points of tidying their room—a chore both young misses regarded with distinct disfavor. It was at this juncture that Harriet Westbrook, her visage alight with the electric thrill of scandal, swept into the room with the drama of a seasoned actress on opening night.

"Charles apprehended by the authorities, can you fathom it?!" Harriet proclaimed, her voice a gale of excitement, as if she were announcing the fall of an empire rather than local gossip.

Elizabeth, momentarily diverted from the stubborn bedsheet she battled, cast a cautionary glance at Harriet. "Mercy, Harriet! Pray, lower your voice— the children," she implored, gesturing toward the intrigued pair, whose interest in the mundane task of room tidying had vanished like mist.

"Ah, of course, my apologies," Harriet murmured, her volume diminished yet her fervor undiminished. "I was just at their tiny little office at the station when I heard. Quite the spectacle, indeed."

Elizabeth smiled, torn between her duties and the gossip. "Really, Harriet? And what did you see there?"

Harriet, unable to contain herself, leaned in closer. "Well, of course, they got the idea from me," she confided with a self-satisfied nod. "Oh Lizzie, I am going to write a book about it. *Tansy Treachery*. But where was I? Yes, well, I heard it from the Reverend that it was Charles who had the tansy, you see. So that was the missing piece to solve this frightful puzzle."

Jenny, wide-eyed and innocent, piped up, "Is Mr. Charles truly wicked, Miss Harriet?"

Caught slightly off-guard by the child's earnest inquiry, Harriet softened her tone. "Well, my dear, that is what the constabulary is set to uncover. It is all quite the mystery."

Elizabeth, sensing the turn of conversation toward realms less suitable for young ears, promptly intervened. "Girls, it's nearing bedtime. Off to wash up," she instructed, her voice firm yet gentle.

"But we wish to hear more of Mr. Charles!" Jenny protested, her curiosity thoroughly piqued.

"Enough dallying. Tomorrow is another day for tales," Elizabeth said, ushering them towards their nightly rituals. The girls reluctantly departed, casting longing glances back at the unfolding adult drama.

Turning back to Harriet, Elizabeth's face mirrored the concern etched in her voice. "Charles? This will weigh heavily on the girls; they are quite fond of him. He always showed them kindness. It's difficult to believe. So has he confessed then?"

Harriet shook her head. "He hasn't confessed to anything, insisted the tansy was for some woman. And then it struck me. Molly was with child. Reginald's," she whispered, eyes on fire. .

Elizabeth gasped, the pieces seeming to fall into place. "So maybe he was afraid of Reginald getting an actual son of his own? Of course, the poor child would have been illegitimate but who knows what Charles was thinking. He was clearly in a bad way."

Harriet nodded, her audience captive. "Precisely, Lizzie. And so I informed the Constable, unveiling the sordid affair right beneath our very noses!" Harriet took a deep breath, a gleam of satisfaction in her eyes. "Just imagine, Lizzie, without our keen observations, those lawmen would be as lost as sailors in the fog. We've practically handed them the solution on a silver platter!"

Elizabeth couldn't help but smile at her friend's unabashed pride. "Indeed, Harriet, your knack for uncovering truths is unparalleled. But now, I really must see to the girls and the rest of the house."

With a reluctant nod, Harriet gathered her shawl. "Of course, duty calls! We shall speak more tomorrow. Goodnight, Elizabeth."

"Goodnight, Harriet," Elizabeth replied, escorting her to the Manor door. As Harriet's footsteps receded into the night, Elizabeth turned to head back to the girls' room.

As she passed through the hallway, the maid Molly Dawson, approached from the opposite direction. Her smile was quick and seemingly genuine, but there was something in it that struck Elizabeth as not quite right—a hint of duplicity, perhaps, or concealed anxiety.

Elizabeth hesitated as Molly's retreating footsteps echoed down the corridor, her mind a tumult of disapproval and concern. *The nerve of that girl, strutting about as though the Manor were her own,* she fumed silently. A child with Reginald, a scandal hidden beneath layers of servility and smiles. It was too much, too reckless. Elizabeth's resolve hardened, and she diverted her path towards the kitchen. The warm, savory scent of the evening's meal still lingered, mingling with the sharp tang of freshly scrubbed pots. Chef Leclair stood at his station, his movements meticulous and rhythmic, a ballet of culinary cleanup.

"Good evening, Chef," Elizabeth greeted, her voice deliberately light, tinged with a feigned nonchalance as she leaned gracefully against the doorway. "Such a day of whispers and winds, wouldn't you say? Ashford seems alive with stories tonight."

Leclair, wiping his hands on a towel, turned with a practiced smile. "Bonsoir, Miss Blythe," he replied, his accent wrapping warmly around his words. "Indeed, the Manor whispers louder than the moors sometimes. What tales fly through the halls tonight?"

Encouraged by his receptive manner, Elizabeth inched closer, lowering her voice. "Actually, it's about Molly—such unsettling news. Harriet just told me... Molly had an affair with Lord Reginald. And had carried his child," she divulged, watching his reaction closely.

The change in Leclair was immediate and startling. The towel slipped from his fingers as his face drained of color, then flushed a deep crimson. His usual poised demeanor cracked, a flash of raw emotion—anger, betrayal—flaring in his eyes. "Mon Dieu," he breathed, the words a hiss of fury and pain. "Is that so?" he managed to say, his voice thick with a barely suppressed rage.

Elizabeth, sensing the depth of his turmoil, continued cautiously, "And, there's more. Harriet learned from the Constable... The pregnancy was ended, apparently with tansy provided by Charles. The Constable has Charles at the station office now."

Leclair's reaction was visceral; his whole body seemed to seize with the impact of the revelation. "Tansy... Charles?" he muttered, almost to himself, as a storm of emotions played across his features. The affable chef of moments ago now stood tense, his hands clenching and unclenching as if grappling with an unseen adversary.

Elizabeth, taken aback by the intensity of his reaction, realized she might have stirred a tempest far greater than anticipated. "I... I thought you should know," she stammered, regret mingling with her concern.

Leclair's expression darkened further, his charming facade crumbling under the weight of the news. "Merci, Miss Blythe," he said stiffly, his tone cold, his posture rigid. "Excuse me, I must see to... to the cleaning."

Startled and fearful of Leclair's reaction, Elizabeth made a hasty retreat. As she hurried from the kitchen, the clatter of pans and the sharp slam of a cupboard marked the chef's struggle to contain his emotions. As she walked away, her mind churned with the implications of her revelation, wondering if she had just lit a fuse that could not be unburnt.

Her heart still pounding from the intense encounter in the kitchen, Elizabeth approached the girls' room. As she reached the door, a sliver of light spilled out onto the hallway floor, a beacon of normalcy in the storm of scandal swirling around the Manor.

Gently, almost reverently, Elizabeth pushed the door open, her eyes scanning the familiar haven with a mix of trepidation and relief. The room lay in quiet repose, bathed in the soft amber glow of the night lamp. Emma and Jenny, nestled in their beds, looked up with expectant eyes, their innocent faces untouched by the storms raging just beyond their peaceful cocoon.

"Can we have a story tonight?" Jenny's voice broke the silence, her words threading through the air like a lifeline thrown in turbulent waters.

"Yes, please," Emma chimed in, her plea soft yet earnest, tugging at Elizabeth's heartstrings.

A sigh of relief escaped Elizabeth as she observed the orderliness of the room—a silent testament to the girls' diligence before their nightly request. Books, their spines aligned like soldiers on parade, stood neatly on the shelf. Toys lay meticulously arranged in their designated nooks, each item in its place. Yet, her eyes soon drifted to a corner where Lady Fluff, the once cherished stuffed rabbit, lay discarded and in disrepair. Its fabric skin was torn, limbs askew, with stuffing entrails spilling out in soft, cottony tufts.

Elizabeth crossed the room and picked up the tattered rabbit, her fingers tracing the seams where playful days had worn the fabric thin. "Poor Lady Fluff has seen better days," she remarked softly, setting the rabbit aside. Turning back to the eager faces of Emma and Jenny, Elizabeth smiled and settled herself comfortably at the foot of their beds. "Well then, what story shall it be tonight?" she asked, her voice weaving a gentle calm over the room's earlier tension.

The girls erupted in a flurry of suggestions and the world outside soon faded, leaving only the soft whispers of characters and the laughter of her young audience.

* * *

Inspector Hargreaves staggered slightly as he reentered the makeshift police office at Goathland train station, the lingering effects of the absinthe tinting his perception with an occasional swirl of colors. He found Constable Barkley standing rigidly, a stoic sentinel over a visibly shaken Charles Windham, who seemed to bear the marks of an interrogation that might have veered too close to zealotry.

Pulling Barkley aside, Hargreaves tried to maintain his composure. The room seemed to pulse subtly, its corners undulating like the gentle waves of a tranquil sea. An occasional flash of color darted at the edge of his vision, reminiscent of the strange specters from Dr. Fletcher's house.

"Dr. Fletcher's analysis was quite thorough, though it yielded little evidence of tansy or other poisons in Lord Reginald's samples," Hargreaves explained, his voice a steady anchor amidst the sensory storm. As he spoke, the shadow of a large moth flitted across the wall, its wings sprawling into grotesque shapes before vanishing into the dim light.

As Hargreaves relayed the doctor's findings, a brief vision of Dr. Fletcher dressed in an exaggerated military uniform flickered before him, complete with a monocle and a baton, gesturing grandly as he discussed his 'reconnaissance missions' into the tissues and fluids of the departed.

Barkley, his brow furrowed in concern, shifted uncomfortably. "I might've been a bit... robust in me questioning of Mr. Windham," he confessed. "Hope the Ashfords don't hold it against me. You did say to be tough, sir," he added, a defensive edge creeping into his voice.

Hargreaves noted the hint of worry that clouded Barkley's features. "Charles did confess, though, said he gave tansy to a woman with child—reckon she was carrying Reginald's," Barkley continued, lowering his voice. "So there's still the matter of a dead baby, sir."

Placing a hand on Barkley's shoulder, Hargreaves sighed. "I always told you to stick by the book, Barkley. You're too fond of playing at the edges." He dismissed Barkley's protests about the infamous nose tap with a wave of his hand. "For both our sakes, after your rather stern chat with Charles, let's not wade unnecessarily into Ashford scandals, especially anything touching on Reginald's illegitimate progeny. Best let that matter—and your friend Charles here—go.."

Barkley nodded, though his expression showed a mix of reluctance and acceptance. "Right, sir. By the book, then, whatever book of yours that may be," he muttered, the uncertainty of their position hung between them like the incoming mist swirling outside.

Approaching Charles, who was slumped in a stark wooden chair, Hargreaves' gaze fell upon the visible signs of a harsh interrogation. Charles' face bore the brutal testimony of the encounter: a lip split to a misshapen thickness, dribbling a slow trickle of blood that had stained his collar, and an eye swollen shut, the surrounding skin painted in harsh hues of purple and yellow. Hargreaves winced slightly, feeling a pang of regret—for Charles and his own career, though not in that order—at the sight.

Under the flickering light of the single gas lamp that did little to illuminate the stark office, Charles' wounds appeared to pulsate with their own malevolent life. The shadows cast by his bruised features danced macabrely on the walls.

"Constable," Hargreaves began, his tone stern, casting a disapproving look at Barkley. "This isn't the toughness I instructed. We are officers of the law, not brutes." His voice carried a mix of reprimand and disappointment, ensuring Charles heard every word.

Turning his attention to Charles, Hargreaves softened his voice. "Mr. Windham, you are free to go," he declared, managing to maintain a composed facade. "I hope you can forgive the… overzealous approach. We are, after all, deeply committed to resolving the tragedy of Lord Reginald's untimely demise."

Charles, grimacing as he rubbed at his swelling eye, was quick to retort as soon as his cuffs were removed. "Forgive? You're both bloody fools," he spat bitterly, standing with a shaky resolve. "I'll have both your badges for this," he promised, his voice thick with anger and indignation.

Attempting to mollify the situation, Hargreaves extended an olive branch. "Allow me to offer you a ride back to Ashford Manor, or wherever you prefer," he suggested, his tone conciliatory.

Charles scoffed, his anger palpable as he backed away from the offer. "I'd rather walk than spend another minute in your company," he declared vehemently, and with those final words, he stormed out of the office into the cool night.

Left in the awkward silence that followed, Hargreaves glanced around the office, the shadows dancing and shifting unnaturally. With a weary sigh, Hargreaves rubbed his temples vigorously, as though he could physically dispel the eerie sensations that clung to his senses like the remnants of a disturbing dream. The musty air of the office mingled with the residual tang of railway soot that seeped in through the poorly sealed windows.

After a moment's uneasy silence, he turned to Barkley, who looked equally unsettled. "Well, Constable, it seems now would be a good time for you to start on that paperwork."

* * *

The night air was crisp as Charles Windham stormed away from the police office, his stride long and fueled by a seething rage. Above him, the sky was a deep velvety black, studded with stars that flickered indifferently to the turmoil below. Yet a mist was beginning to roll in from the moors, cloaking the landscape in a ghostly shroud that seemed to echo his current state of mind—clouded, with a growing chill of dread.

As he followed the railway tracks, a path lit only by the sporadic glow of distant lamplights and the silvery gleam of the moon, Charles's inner thoughts churned with a tumultuous fury. The indignity of his arrest, the rough hands and harsh words of Constable Barkley, and the condescending tones of Inspector Hargreaves—all these imprinted a vow within him to exact a heavy price from those men. Yet, as his anger boiled, his thoughts inevitably spiraled back to Amelia. The tansy—the subject of the lawmen's accusation but also the source of his most current worry. Amelia had taken it hours ago, and the promise he had made now haunted him. It was well beyond the time he had vowed to return to her side.

His breath quickened with each step, mist forming clouds around him as he exhaled in the cold night air. He remembered the Inspector's offer—the carriage that could have hastened his return. Yet, the very idea of accepting a ride, of possibly leading them to Amelia's refuge, was unthinkable. His movements had to remain his own, untracked.

As Charles continued his solitary trek along the railway tracks, a prickling sensation of being watched crept over him. The night was quiet, too quiet, and every sound seemed amplified—a distant rustle, the soft thud of footsteps. He quickened his pace, but the sounds mirrored his urgency. Turning abruptly, his eyes squinted into the darkness, and there, not far behind, was the dim glow of a lantern swaying with the gait of its bearer.

"Who are you? Why do you follow me?" Charles called out, his voice echoing off the silent trees flanking the railway.

A hollow, despondent laugh cut through the night air as the figure stepped closer, the light revealing his features. "Monsieur Charles, I have served you many meals, yet you do not recognize me?" The man's voice was thick with a French accent, tinged with a chilling mirth.

Charles stared at the approaching figure, recognition dawning slowly. It was Leclair, the chef from Ashford Manor, but there was something deeply unsettling in his demeanor tonight. His eyes gleamed unnaturally in the lantern light, and his smile was twisted by a dark grief.

"I do not make it my business to memorize every face in the kitchens," Charles retorted sharply, his words laced with an aristocratic disdain.

Leclair's laugh turned into a snarl. "Ah, Monsieur, toujours la même arrogance! You, who are handed everything on a silver platter, must still take, and take, and take!" His voice rose, each word punctuated with a bitter vehemence.

As Leclair advanced, Charles noticed the gleam of metal in his hand—a knife, a chef's sabatier, already stained with dark spots that were unmistakably blood. Leclair set the lantern down beside the tracks and held up the knife, its blade catching the moonlight.

"Regardez bien, Monsieur," Leclair hissed, his eyes burning with a wild intensity. He held up the sabatier, the blade glinting malevolently under the moon's pale light. "Behold, this sabatier, forged with the utmost precision—its balance perfect, its edge razor-sharp. A chef's prized tool."

Leclair's fingers traced the steel lovingly, his voice dropping to a menacing murmur as he approached Charles. "I've used this very knife to carve the finest cuts, you know. Many a dish served up to you. A tenderloin, sliced thin enough to melt on the tongue; a brisket, separated from the bone with nothing more than a flick of the wrist."

With each step closer, his description grew more vivid, the edge of threat in his voice sharpening. "And then there are the tougher cuts, those that require a bit more... force," Leclair continued. "The cleave through a joint, the severing of sinew—each stroke deliberate, decisive. Just like I am being now, Monsieur Charles."

The knife danced lightly in his hand as if to demonstrate, slicing through the air with an effortless grace that belied its deadly potential. "Tonight it is not veal or lamb under the blade's judgment, but something far more treacherous." Leclair's smile twisted cruelly as he closed the distance, the cold steel of the sabatier promising nothing but dark intentions. "You are not a lamb, are you Monsieur Charles? No, a wolf among the sheep."

Charles, realizing the peril he was in, took a step back, his heart pounding as he faced the enraged chef and the sharp promise of the blade glinting ominously in the dim light.

As Leclair menacingly advanced, his silhouette was edged by the dim glow of the lantern left on the side of the tracks. Charles stumbled backward, his eyes locked on the glinting sabatier. Leclair's voice was low, laced with accusation and a cold, piercing anger that cut deeper than the night's chill.

"Dis-moi, Charles, did she tell you whose child it was? Was it mine? Reginald's? Or perhaps," Leclair's tone dropped, venomous and accusing, "it was yours? Was she sleeping with you too, playing me the fool all along?"

Charles, his back nearly against the cold metal of a railway signal, responded with a blend of anger and bafflement. "I don't know who you're talking about. I have no interest in the dramas of servants," he said, his voice dripping with condescension.

Leclair's expression twisted into one of fury mixed with pain as he hissed back, "I know about the tansy you gave to Molly. You'll regret feeding me more lies!" His advance was relentless, the knife a constant threat in his unsteady hand.

"I hardly know Molly," Charles retorted sharply, his voice rising in panic and irritation. "She's just one of many who might polish my shoes. If you're so desperate to know who fathered her child, why don't you ask her yourself?"

For the first time, Leclair halted, his advance stopping as his shoulders slumped slightly. "It's too late to ask Molly any more questions," he said softly, a sorrowful edge creeping into his voice. Charles noted again the blood staining the knife—an ominous testament to the chef's words.

Leclair's figure, framed by the lantern's pale fire, seemed to sag as the reality of his words settled between them. The night air, thick with mist and tension, carried his soft, despairing whisper. "It is too late for any questions now. Too late for anything but this."

Leclair, with a swift and sudden movement, slashed at Charles with his blade aimed directly across Charles' face. Reacting just in time, Charles whipped his head back, feeling the cold sting of the blade grazing his cheek, a line of warm blood tracing down his skin.

"Ah, le sang," Leclair murmured darkly, eyeing the blood with a grotesque fascination. "Just like that night. Was it the tansy that did it? So much blood. I'll spill your blood just like you spilled the child's blood." His voice was heavy with accusation, his eyes wild.

The mention of blood, the tansy, brought a visceral image to Charles' mind—Amelia in distress, alone, possibly bleeding out just like Molly had. The thought injected a fierce surge of adrenaline through him, igniting a desperate fury to return to her side.

As the eerie sound of a distant train horn cut through the night, its warning light began to illuminate the tracks, casting long, dancing shadows around them. Leclair raised the knife again, his arm tensed for a deadly strike. Charles, driven by a mix of fear and rage, intercepted the blade with his hand, feeling its vicious bite deep into his flesh. But the shock of his countermove stunned Leclair.

Seizing the moment, Charles landed a solid punch with his free hand to Leclair's face, knocking him off balance. Fueled by his swirling emotions and the pulsing pain in his hand, Charles didn't stop. He pummeled Leclair with his fist, driving him back along the tracks.

They grappled fiercely, stumbling over each other until they both fell onto the tracks, the knife clattering away into the darkness. Charles, nearly blind to his own bleeding and the searing pain, kept striking, each blow fueled by the haunting image of Amelia alone in a blood soaked bed amidst the overwhelming sound of the approaching train. The horn blared again, closer now, its light almost blinding.

In the frenzied moments that followed, Charles's survival instincts kicked in. With a final push, he hurled himself from the tracks just as the train thundered past, its force pulling at his clothes and hair. He rolled to safety, his breath ragged, his body aching.

Turning back, he saw that Leclair had not managed to escape. The train, a massive, unstoppable force, rushed by, a mere blur of light and sound, the angry blaring horn and Leclair's death scream merging as one.

After a few moments spent lying on the cold, damp earth, Charles gathered what little strength he had left and staggered to his feet. He picked up the lantern Leclair had left on the side of the tracks. Pain radiated from his wounds. Each step towards Ashford Manor was a battle against the drain of his energy and the loss of blood that marked his path like breadcrumbs.

Finally, after what seemed like hours later, the manor loomed ahead, its walls a ghostly silhouette under the moonlit sky. As he neared, a flickering lantern light caught his eye, glowing from a window on the side of the grand house. Desperate to reach the stables and take the stallion to ride to the cottage where Amelia awaited, he maintained his course passing by the side of the manor, his body on the brink of collapse.

As he passed the window, a voice shattered the silence. "Who goes there?" it called out, wary and tense.

Charles, his senses dulled by pain and fatigue, barely processed the question. In no state to run, he approached, leaned closer to the window, squinting to make out the figures inside. Recognition dawned just as he reached the glass, and in a moment of delirious confusion mixed with reflexive instinct, he murmured, "Boo!" as he raised the lantern up to the level of his face.

At Charles's ghostly figure—his face a tapestry of cuts, his clothes torn and bloodied, and his bones setting at unnatural angles—the screams of Jenny, Emma, and Elizabeth Blythe pierced the night air. Elizabeth clutched the girls close, her eyes wide with horror at the sight of him, transformed into something barely recognizable.

Charles tried to speak, to explain, but his voice was a raspy whisper, lost in the echoes of their screams.

CHAPTER 7
A FAR BETTER REST

In the heart of York, many miles removed from the violent intrigues and hallucinogenic excesses that recently convulsed the North York Moors, Julian Ashford found himself far from at ease in his grand administrative office. As the grand clock chimed, marking the late hour, Julian faced Inspector Hargreaves and Constable Barkley, who awaited his address with a mix of anticipation and unease. Mr. Harrowgate, always impeccably attired, was admirably fulfilling his role of being present and thereby lending an air of legal solemnity to the assembly.

Julian's initial cordiality was a thin veil, his impatience palpable. "Gentlemen, thank you for assembling on such short notice," he started, his voice tinged with a frost that matched the evening chill seeping through the high windows. "We are to conclude this investigation, then? Assigning blame to a deceased servant seems a rather facile resolution. Convenient, isn't it? And yet, the real culprit remains the stewardess of the estate."

His fingers drummed a staccato rhythm on the oak surface of his desk, a physical manifestation of his frustration. "This tidy closure you propose, is it not simply an attempt to sweep true issues under the rug?" Julian challenged, his gaze piercing.

Mr. Harrowgate, standing slightly apart with his hands clasped behind his back, interjected with his typical rhetorical method. "What is our paramount duty in this matter? To leap to conclusions, or to proceed with precision and discretion?" He paused, with a sharp look directed at Julian. "We must anchor our actions in evidence, not the quicksands of mere suspicion."

Julian raised a hand to forestall any further platitudes. "Evidence, Mr. Harrowgate, is precisely what I demand." He paused, turning to face Hargreaves and Barkley. "Inspector, Constable, I implore you to elaborate how you've reached such a neat conclusion amidst such a convoluted affair," he pressed, his voice low but clear.

Inspector Hargreaves cleared his throat, gathering his thoughts under the stern gaze of Julian Ashford. "Mr. Ashford, the conclusions we've drawn are not taken lightly nor made in haste. Our investigation has been thorough and meticulous, covering every angle of this distressing case."

Constable Barkley chimed in. "Well, it all clicked soon enough, it did. Turns out we had a raving lunatic right in the kitchens the whole time; killed poor Molly, he did, and was fixing to do in your cousin Charles too."

Hargreaves continued, "Yes, Charles Windham was attacked by none other than Henri Leclair, the chef at the Manor. Leclair, wielding the same knife used on the maid Molly Dawon, admitted in the heat of confrontation that he couldn't stand the thought of Molly and Lord Reginald together."

Julian leaned forward, his skepticism not just evident but sharply defined. "And this is what you consider conclusive? A chef, suddenly a lunatic, confessing under the duress of a violent outburst? This is the foundation on which you've built your case?" He waved dismissively, his tone laden with incredulity. "Servant squabbles and sensational tales—headline fodder, nothing more. I'm supposed to believe that this chef, who you claim dispatched the lord of the manor with such stealth as to evade notice, suddenly erupts into a murderous frenzy a week later? Why this delayed fury? If he knew of an affair and killed my brother for it, why kill Molly only now? It stretches credulity, gentlemen."

Feeling the weight of the scrutiny and the sting of Julian's dismissive attitude, Constable Barkley bristled. "Just how many blasted murderers do you reckon we have lurking about Ashford Manor, eh? Not satisfied with catching one, is that it?!"

Inspector Hargreaves, aiming to diffuse the growing tension, intervened with a calm, measured tone. "Mr. Ashford, while your concerns are understandable, we cannot overlook the fact that Henri Leclair has indisputably committed murder. With two tragic deaths in such short succession at Ashford Manor, the probability that he is responsible for both is far higher than the likelihood of another murderer at large. Moreover, as the estate's chef, he would have had ample opportunity to administer poison to Lord Reginald discreetly. True, we do not know what poison was used. Further, we cannot pinpoint the exact moment he discovered the alleged affair, but only a week has passed since Lord Reginald's demise, and we have learned that Molly had taken leave to visit her family, only to return after your brother's death. During this period, Mr. Leclair's behavior has been increasingly erratic, demonstrating his instability."

Julian, still unconvinced, arched an eyebrow, his skepticism not abated. "So are we to just ignore the other evidence then? That my brother was preparing to change his will right before his untimely passing, and that—that woman had everything to lose but has now gained everything?"

At this point, Mr. Harrowgate interjected. "Is it not more plausible that a man on the edge of reason, faced with betrayals either real or perceived, might indeed collapse under the strain? Other than the mere fact that she is now stewardess of the estate, there has been no evidence uncovered that Lady

Eleanor had any connection to the murder."

The room grew tense as Julian Ashford continued to probe the conclusions presented by the lawmen. With a look of deep contemplation and evident dissatisfaction, he posed another question. "So, what of this attack on Charles, then? How did that factor into your culprit's grand maniacal designs?"

Inspector Hargreaves exchanged a brief, significant glance with Constable Barkley before responding. "Well, it indeed left Mr. Windham rather shaken, not to mention bruised and battered"—he paused to glance briefly at Barkley again—"being attacked so suddenly. It seems, however," he continued, choosing his words carefully, "that Leclair was under the impression—or delusion—that Molly carried Lord Reginald's child and that Mr. Windham played a role in some tragic misfortune concerning the unborn." The Inspector and Constable exchanged yet another look. "It is our opinion that Leclair acted alone while under certain mental delusions and naturally we do not see a need to inquire into that matter further, or make details of his delusions public."

Julian's expression soured as if tasting something particularly bitter. "It scarcely seems plausible," he muttered. "But yes, the man does seem to have been out of his mind. His little adventure on the tracks caused a bit of delay—did you know?" He sighed. "The train was seventeen minutes late departing the next station. Seventeen minutes, but we made it up eventually. Progress," he added with a rueful hint of pride, "moves ever forward."

Yet, Julian's expression hardened again. "No," he said firmly, his jaw set in a determined line, "I told you at the beginning, this ends when you solve the murder *correctly* and arrest Lady Eleanor."

Constable Barkley muttered under his breath, looking between Julian and Hargreaves, "Oi, shouldn't he be tapping his nose, to make it proper, like?"

Inspector Hargreaves addressed Julian with a firm resolve. "We have conducted our investigation meticulously and by the book. We've tied up the case with the culprit already dealt with. However, it's crucial to note there's scant evidence that Lord Reginald was deliberately murdered. Imagine the potential scandal and upheaval—initiating a prolonged investigation, halting his burial—all potentially for naught if it turned out to be mere natural causes. All the more scandalous, I am sure I need not remind you, if the only purported evidence is one family member's grievance over the terms of the will. The resolution we have may appear hollow, but it's a victory in ensuring minimal embarrassment for the family and, further,"—here the Inspector's eyes gleamed with his own pride—"maintaining bureaucratic integrity."

As Julian fidgeted irritably, clearly unappeased by Hargreaves' rationale, his glower deepened, signaling his continued dissatisfaction.

Breaking the growing tension, Mr. Harrowgate stepped forward, his voice calm but authoritative. "What is the expression? When one door closes, another opens. If Lady Eleanor is not to be led to the executioner, might she not be led to the altar? Perhaps to her late husband's brother?" The suggestion hung in the air.

Julian's expression morphed into contemplative. The idea seemed to churn in his mind as he chewed on it forcefully, his demeanor shifting from combative to pensive. At Julian's silence, Mr. Harrowgate delivered the coup de grace with his usual rhetorical flair. "And is not marriage, gentlemen, the very epitome of progress—two souls forging ahead on a united path?" He smiled wryly. "What better way to honor the past and secure the future than by binding it with the bonds of matrimony?" At this, Julian's jaw came to rest, and he allowed himself a smile.

* * *

And so we return once again to Ashford Manor, that grand stage upon which yet another performance of mourning unfolds for the late Lord Reginald. Having rehearsed this somber act once before, the ensemble might have perfected the art of grief; yet, this time, their display carried an undercurrent of "let's just get on with it." Indeed, on this day the heavens themselves chose restraint, not deigning to weep. The sun, bold and unrepentant, bathed the estate in a lavish golden light, slicing through the morning's crispness over the moors with audacious clarity. Nature itself seemed to conspire to signal the dawn of a new era for Ashford Manor.

Leading the procession with a demeanor of composed sovereignty was Lady

Eleanor Ashford. Still adorned in the customary garb of mourning, her attire whispered of solemnity yet screamed of authority. Her strides were more decisive than in days past, each step a firm imprint upon the paths of her realm. The black lace of her veil, once a curtain to shield her grief, now fluttered in the breeze like a banner proclaiming her ascendance in the estate's hierarchy.

Flanking Lady Eleanor, young Jenny and Emma, shepherded by the ever-vigilant Elizabeth Blythe, advanced with a decorous mix of curiosity and solemnity. A few paces behind, Charles Windham moved with a palpable heaviness. The once dashing figure, brimming with an easy arrogance, now bore the marks of recent trials—his visage scarred, his demeanor that of a man recalibrating his presence within his own skin.

Not far from this chastened soul, Julian Ashford made his presence known, his every step marked by a resolved determination.

As the mournful procession snaked its way toward the open grave, Reverend Smythe stood sentinel by the gaping chasm. The flush of his cheeks, rosier than the morning's kiss upon the moors, might have been credited to the chill of early day—or perhaps to the generous fortification of wine that had braced him against the day's somber duties.

The Reverend cleared his throat, a sound that rumbled through the quiet like distant thunder. "We are convened once again in this hallowed cradle of repose to bestow upon Lord Reginald Ashford the final benediction that eludes no man," he began. His eyes fluttered shut, perhaps in reverence, or perhaps to steady the swaying landscape his libations had conjured—libations which had not fully quited his inner tumult. Memories of recent confidences shared in earnest haunted him—Molly Dawson's tearful recounting of Lord Reginald's ungentlemanly advances painted a sordid picture starkly at odds with the sanctified praises now expected of him. He wrestled momentarily with the hypocrisy of his role, the taste of wine bitter on his tongue.

"As Solomon wisely declared in Ecclesiastes, 'To everything there is a season, and a time to every purpose under the heaven,'" Smythe intoned. "A time to be born, and a time to die; a time to plant, and a time to pluck up that which is planted. Today, we gather not just to mourn, but to reflect on the inevitable journey we all must undertake."

"As we lay to rest one whose life was cut short under shadows of suspicion and sorrow, let us remember that even in the darkest of tales, the light of truth eventually illuminates. We must not let our hearts be troubled by the specters of what might have been, nor should we dwell in the valley of the shadow of doubt," he intoned. Charles Windham shifted uncomfortably, feeling the brief gaze of many eyes upon him.

"Let us then commit his body to the ground; earth to earth, ashes to ashes, dust to dust; in sure and certain hope of the Resurrection to eternal life," Reverend Smythe declared. "While Lord Reginald's rest was abruptly but briefly delayed, it is now a far, far better rest that he goes to than he has ever known." His eyes opened, fixing upon the crowd with an intensity. "And joining in this moment today I see brilliant people rising from this abyss of grief and uncertainty, gathered here in testament to the enduring spirit of community and faith."

Reverend Smythe concluded, "And so, we release our beloved Reginald to the arms of the earth, trusting that today's sorrow seeds tomorrow's hope." The casket descended solemnly into the earth, the finality of the act punctuated by the soft thud of sod against the polished wood, a stark reminder that, in the end, all are equal in the dust.

As the last echoes of the service faded, Smythe, slightly unsteady but satisfied with his delivery, quietly recited to himself, "When it is red, when it sparkles in a cup, when it goes down smoothly." A wry smile played upon his lips, his duty discharged, his spirit buoyed by the sacred and the profane alike.

Charles Windham turned abruptly from the newly filled grave, an instinctive motion drawing his fingers to the scar marring his face—a constant reminder of recent horrors. His touch lingered as if to confirm the reality of the mark, the whispers and sidelong glances from the crowd—sometimes real, sometimes imagined—only intensifying his discomfort. Across the sea of mourners, his gaze momentarily met Amelia Rutherford's. Her eyes, once warm with affection, flicked away almost immediately.

Nearby, Harriet Westbrook leaned close to Elizabeth Blythe. Her voice, though hushed to respect the solemnity of the occasion, vibrated with her customary excitement. "Elizabeth, can you believe it? The whole saga has finally come to an end with Henri Leclair!" She glanced around, ensuring the propriety of their conversation given young Emma and Jenny's proximity. "It was the dashing chef with the culinary cutlery after all! I'm thinking of calling the book *Killer in the Kitchen.*. It's got a ring, don't you think?" Her eyes sparkled with the thrill of the tale, her earlier misjudgments of Charles now just a minor footnote to the story she was eager to tell.

"I was indeed wrong about Charles," Harriet confessed with a mixture of concession and pride. "Yet, it was my keen observations that unraveled this twisted tale! Imagine, Leclair, consumed by such dark jealousy!" As she reveled in recounting the dramatic downfall of Leclair and the tragic end of poor Molly, Elizabeth's response was more muted than usual. The memory of Leclair's transformation before her eyes haunted her.

As Harriet continued, Elizabeth's attention was drawn away by Jenny's soft sobbing, the young girl overwhelmed by the somber reality of the grave. "Excuse me, Harriet," Elizabeth murmured, her voice tinged with weariness as she turned to comfort Jenny, yet grateful for any distraction from Harriet's retelling of Molly's death.

Across the cemetery, Julian Ashford was navigating through the crowd with a determined stride towards Lady Eleanor. He deftly sidestepped Reverend Smythe, who offered his modestly slurred condolences. Julian only nodded politely, his mind preoccupied with crafting the perfect opening line to Lady Eleanor. He rehearsed silently, reshaping his words to present himself as the gallant, sensible brother of her late husband, ready to offer stability—and yes, progress—to Ashford Manor.

As Julian continued his approach, Harriet Westbrook swooped in, her voice ringing with a blend of mournful joy. "Mr. Ashford, such a poignant pleasure to see you again, albeit under such sorrowful skies!" she gushed, clinging to his sleeve with a fervor that belied the somber setting. "Any updates on the stewardship of the estate? In such trying times, your leadership is surely the beacon we all seek."

Julian's smile, strained and polite, thinly veiled his annoyance. "Not now, Harriet. There are duties to which I must attend," he replied, extricating himself with a courtesy that barely masked his haste. Under his breath, he muttered, "Ever the sleuth, aren't we, Harriet?"

Scarcely had he escaped Harriet's clutches than Dr. Fletcher appeared, holding court among a cluster of mourners. "Ah, Julian! A tragic day, indeed! Lord Reginald fought valiantly against the cruel fates, as a soldier at his post!" boomed the doctor.

Julian offered a brisk nod, his response automatic. "Indeed, Doctor, the very paragon of bravery," he concurred, sidestepping the doctor to resume his mission. With each step towards Lady Eleanor, his mental rehearsals became increasingly grandiose.

"Lady Eleanor," he practiced under his breath, "in these turbulent times, Ashford Manor stands in need of resolute leadership. Who better to provide it than the brother of your esteemed late husband? Together, we shall right the ship of this storied estate, guiding it to a future as glorious as its past."

His fantasies grew bolder with each paced rehearsal. In a particularly vivid daydream, he imagined Lady Eleanor praising his fortitude and greeting him with a wistful sigh. "Oh, Julian, what solace your presence brings! And such a full head of hair you maintain!" Julian's hand instinctively rose to pat the thinning crown of his head, a self-satisfied grin spreading across his face as he savored the comforting fabric of his own illusions.

Perhaps it is easy enough for these mourners to overlook that the North York Moors cradle more than one newly turned patch of earth, but, dear reader, we need not share in that oversight. The North York Moors is scattered with freshly hollowed and hallowed grounds. Aye, just at the border of the vast Ashford estate, one might still spot that smaller plot, modestly adorned with fading wildflowers—red, yellow, and blue. Their vibrant hues now surrender to the inevitable fade of time, no longer refreshed by the daily tributes of grieving hands. This unmarked grave whispers of a simpler life and quieter departures, its resident's secrets forever held close beneath the cold North York soil.

In the humble confines of St. Mary's Parish Cemetery, a modest marker etched merely with the name 'Molly Dawson' rests amongst the unassuming graves of common folk. Here, her parents, clad in the worn fabric of workaday life, have laid simple tokens of remembrance—a small wooden cross, a few personal trinkets evoking memories of a life taken too soon. Their quiet mourning, devoid of opulence, speaks a stark truth about the fleeting nature of remembrance in a world where grand legacies overshadow simple stories.

Meanwhile, in a far more desolate part of this earth, at a forgotten corner of the York County Pauper's Cemetery, lies Henri Leclair. His final resting place, a nondescript plot in a field of the unnamed and unwanted, bears no mark to hint at the man's turbulent ending. It is a grave befitting those cast out from society, a stark repository for souls departed under the shadow of infamy. Here, the wind whispers not of grief or fond remembrance but of the chill indifference reserved for those whose lives ended under the shadow of disgrace.

The land holds all these souls in its embrace, yet to each a disparate resting place, separated by class and circumstance. One might ponder if the spirits might find each other in the vast expanse of eternity. Yet, for Leclair, weighed down by sins too heavy for redemption, the prospect of familial reunion in the hereafter may elude him as thoroughly in death as it did in life. Indeed, in death as in life, the bonds that may or may not have united them remain a mystery deeply buried, their secrets held tight by the sanctity of the grave.

* * *

Under the encroaching shroud of twilight, the Boulby Cliffs stood as a forbidding monument against the vast expanse of the North Sea. Stark, sheer, and unyielding, they cut a formidable silhouette against the rapidly darkening sky. Below, the relentless waves clashed against the cliff base with a mournful roar that seemed to tell of desolation and the eternal struggle between sea and stone. The salty spray, mingling with the chill wind, carried the faint, ghostly whispers of ancient, sunken secrets lost in the unfathomable depths below.

These cliffs, known for their dizzying heights, held tales of smugglers who once deftly navigated the shadowy coves and hidden caves beneath. These caverns, sculpted by the tireless sea over countless millennia, had served as secret vaults for contraband—ranging from French brandy to opulent silks— shrouded in the cliffs' formidable embrace. With time, they bore witness to innumerable vessels ensnared by their treacherous allure, each shipwreck adding another layer to the cliffs' legendary mystique.

On this particular evening, the atmosphere was laden with the scent of impending rain, and seabirds circled like ghostly sentinels overhead. Their piercing cries added to the haunting symphony of wind and water. Amidst this dramatic natural cathedral of towering stone and churning sea, a lone figure on horseback appeared.

Charles, astride a stalwart stallion, approached the precipice with a pace that was deliberate and measured. The rhythmic beat of the horse's hooves against the hard, cold ground echoed ominously, mirroring the quiet despair enveloping him like a heavy cloak. As each hoof struck stone, the echo mingled with the thunderous clash of the waves below.

Haunted by the scars of recent ordeals—both physical and emotional— Charles contemplated the severed ties that now marked his existence. Why had Amelia turned from him, when he had so desperately sought her support? His marred visage, a grim testament to his suffering, seemed to repel her, transforming him in her eyes from beloved to beast.

In the village, some whispered heroics about him, but Charles felt the hollowness of such accolades. To Amelia, his presence was now akin to that of a specter—there, yet unacknowledged. Was it his appearance that repelled her, or was it the scandalous whispers that shadowed him relentlessly?

"Molly!" The name was a specter that haunted him, an unwelcome shadow that linked him to a tragedy he had barely touched yet seemed irrevocably tied to. With each step towards the cliff's edge, the wind seemed to strip away layers of his resolve, leaving his soul bare and shivering against the raw power of the elements.

The cliffs stood indifferent to his turmoil, their ancient faces worn yet resolute against the ages. Charles paused, feeling the pull of the abyss before him. His horse, sensing its master's distress, snorted nervously. Below, the waves crashed with unyielding ferocity, indifferent to human suffering, a relentless force of nature that carved rock and fate with the same dispassionate might. Here at the precipice was the divide between the abyss and the unforgiving world behind him.

The chill wind tore at Charles as he dismounted near the precipice, his boots crunching on the gravel, each step a resolute echo in the twilight silence. He stood at the cliff's edge, gazing into the encroaching gloom where the North Sea churned below, its restless waves a dark mirror to his tormented thoughts. The cold sea spray lashed against him, each drop mingling with the bitter reality of his financial ruin.

His mind, a whirlpool of grim calculations, turned relentlessly over the sums of his debts. They were the dismal legacy of ill-fated investments and reckless nights at the gambling tables in Manchester, where each wager was placed with the desperate hope that luck would, at last, turn in his favor. Even the drastic measure of selling his cousin's prized stallions—save the last remaining horse that was his sole companion now—had ultimately been a futile gesture, barely making a dent in the vast ocean of his obligations. The money raised was trifling against the enormity of his debts, and the realization that he would still be hounded by creditors was as harsh and chilling as the wind scouring the cliffs.

Living on the run from debt collectors was no true life; it was mere existence, a shadowy survival in a perpetual state of flight, with no sanctuary to be found. As he stood there, the memories of a different time began to filter through the fog of his current despair—recollections of an adolescence steeped in opulence, where every luxury and whim seemed but a hand's reach away.

It was during those formative years at the manor, under the watchful eyes of surrogate parents who, though generous, never quite acknowledged him or Amelia as their own, that the thefts began. What started as a childish game between him and Amelia—stealing trinkets from around the manor that were rarely missed—soon evolved into their secret contest. They bestowed upon each other the spoils of their silent conquests, a game that paralleled their burgeoning, clandestine flirtations.

As they grew, so too did the seriousness of their thefts. Several of Lady Eleanor's jewels had found their way into Amelia's hands, gifted by Charles in a twisted expression of affection and alliance. Amelia, in turn, gifted him with valuables, which he often took back to Manchester to sell or pawn—fuel for the fires of his gambling and debt.

This cycle of theft and gift became an addiction, a habit neither could break even as adults. It was a claim, a rebellion against the very adults who raised them yet held them at arm's length—never truly theirs in the ways that mattered.

With each crashing wave below, Charles felt the weight of his past decisions more acutely, the echoes of those stolen joys now shadows that danced mockingly in the spray. The thefts, once thrilling, now seemed hollow, empty gestures in the face of the immense consequences they had wrought. His mind involuntarily conjured the ghastly visage of Henri Leclair in their last, violent encounter. It was the face of a man who had nothing left to lose, marked by an expression of desperate, cornered fury—the same look that haunted Charles not just in his nightmares, but in his reflections in every mirror.

The reason behind Leclair's frenzied attack on him remained shrouded in layers of rage and madness. The common whispers painted Leclair as a man unhinged by jealousy and loss, driven to exterminate not only Molly but Charles as well, believing him to be another of Reginald's protectors, or worse, another rival in his delusional battle for Molly's affection. And yet, amid these swirling accusations and the terror of Leclair's blade, Charles bore the heavy, solitary burden of a darker truth: Leclair had not killed Lord Reginald.

As the chilling wind buffeted him, Charles's thoughts were inexorably drawn to the fateful day of Reginald's death—a memory he sought to suppress, yet found himself powerless to banish. He remembered the silver snuff box in his hand, caught in the act by Reginald in his own study—a foolish risk, borne of mounting recklessness as his debts spiraled. His attempted levity had fallen flat, for Reginald had already been piecing together the betrayal, his suspicion ignited days earlier upon seeing Amelia accidentally adorned with Lady Eleanor's pendant.

The confrontation that ensued had been volcanic. Reginald accused Charles of the ultimate betrayal, not just of his trust, but of their familial bonds, tainted by the illicit, barely concealed affections between Charles and Amelia. As Reginald's anger seethed to a fearsome pitch, he revealed his plans to excise Charles from his will, and to banish both him and Amelia from Ashford Manor forever. Amidst the fury and accusations, Charles had stood frozen, the weight of his choices crashing down upon him as Reginald vowed to sever all ties.

"Fine. You are not my son. She is not my daughter. That's what you want to hear, right?" Reginald had bellowed, his voice seething with fury. "Neither of you have any place at Ashford Manor. I never want to see either of you again." He spat out his words with a venomous intensity.

But suddenly, Reginald's face contorted in pain, his hands clutching at his chest as his breath became labored. He gasped for air, his body weakened by the sudden heart failure, his hand reaching out towards Charles—not in anger, but in a desperate plea for help. Charles, caught in a tempest of shock and rising panic, had found himself momentarily frozen, his feet rooted to the spot as Reginald struggled before him. Then, as if watching himself from afar, Charles moved towards Reginald, and then passed him. He retrieved a pillow from the study sofa, his movements calm and methodical.

Approaching the gasping Reginald, Charles had used one arm to prop him slightly while he positioned the pillow against Reginald's face. The act was chilling in its quiet efficiency, smothering any sounds of struggle or remaining breath. They maintained the grim embrace for what felt like an eternity, Charles feeling an eerie calm as he held the pillow in place. Finally, Charles realized that Reginald's struggles had ceased, his body limp and unresponsive. Gently, he had moved Reginald onto the sofa, returned the pillow, and exited the study with silver snuff box in hand.

The numbness that had cushioned him during the dreadful act against Reginald and in the days that followed had dissolved, leaving behind only raw, searing pain. Some of this grief was for Reginald, indeed, but more overwhelmingly, it was for himself—for the path he had trodden, now culminating at this precipice of despair.

Peering into the churning waters, Charles recalled Amelia's once-sweet vision: "A little house by the sea...you and me." The memory, once a beacon of hope, now twisted into a cruel mockery by the harsh winds of reality. The dream they had woven together was irrevocably shattered, leaving behind nothing but the cold embrace of the ocean.

"The ocean is so freeing," she had said, her voice echoed in his mind, a ghostly whisper swept away by the wind. With a heavy heart, Charles contemplated the final step, a step that would end the torment of his haunted memories and the weight of his guilt. The ocean, indifferent and eternal, called to him, promising oblivion, promising peace.

With a last, lingering look at the darkening skies above and the relentless sea below, Charles stepped forward, surrendering to the path he had carved for himself. His form fell, then disappeared into the abyss, swallowed by the night and the waves, welcoming another errant smuggler home.

CHAPTER 8
THE BEST OF TIMES

And so we arrive at last at our happy ending. Lord Reginald has been finally laid to rest, his murderer vanquished. But what of those that remain?

What tales, for instance, yet linger in the bustling corridors of life for our steadfast Inspector Hargreaves and his loyal Constable Barkley?

The duo, whose exploits have now become the stuff of local legend—if not without a generous dusting of bureaucratic embellishment—find themselves rapidly ascending the ladder of constabulary bureaucracy. Inspector Hargreaves, adorned with a new title that necessitated the engraving of several new door plates, reveled in the glow of justice served. Constable Barkley, now also promoted to a supervisory role, discovered the unexpected charm of overseeing others as they trudged through the muck and mire of fieldwork.

Indeed, the erstwhile perils of their law enforcement pursuits have been supplanted by the daunting precipices of paperwork. "Look at us now, guv," Barkley remarked, casting a sweeping gesture towards their desks, now beleaguered under a deluge of documents. "From chasin' villains to chasin' signatures. It's a bloomin' different sort of marathon, innit?"

"A veritable marathon, indeed," Hargreaves responded, his eyes eagerly scanning the various pamphlets and forms laid out in front of him.

"Jenkins!" Barkley bellowed robustly to a young officer whose face was suddenly awash with anxiety, "you're to fetch Tommy 'the Twitch' from the market square for a friendly chat, eh?"

"And you, Simmons," he continued, turning to another youthful recruit. "Give 'em the old switcheroo. Present him with a scowl fierce enough to curdle milk, let him know we're not here to sell biscuits."

Simmons, invigorated by the directive, began to scribble with the urgency of a scribe in the queen's court. Barkley leaned forward to deliver the grand finale. "And when you've got 'im all rattled, you scarper out, and Jenkins here will swoop in, all smiles and comfort. Watch, he'll sing like a canary before you can knock back a pint."

Barkley's commands ricocheted off the high walls, while Hargreaves added his own sonorous admonition, "And don't forget, lads, dot the 'i's and cross the 't's on those forms! It's all in the details! Precision! Decorum! By the book, now!"

As the room settled back into the rhythmic scratching of pens against paper, Hargreaves and Barkley exchanged a look of mutual contentment. "Oi, to the best of times, eh?" Barkley raised an imaginary glass in salute to their victories and the quiet life of paperwork that now lay before them.

Elsewhere, Reverend Smythe and Dr. Fletcher were sharing drinks out of decidedly non-imaginary glasses. To their delight, the frictions of church and science were not of such magnitude that they could not be resolved over a drink or two or three. This evening, while at Dr. Fletcher's curious abode, the two embarked on a spirited exploration of one particularly notorious beverage—absinthe.

"Behold, Reverend, the liberator of minds!" Dr. Fletcher proclaimed with a flourish, unleashing the verdant spirit from its glass confines. His eyes sparkled with the thrill of forbidden science as he prepared their glasses with an almost liturgical precision.

Reverend Smythe, ever the pious observer, regarded the emerald draught with a mixture of awe and apprehension. "Indeed, Doctor, they speak of spirits in the Good Book, but none so potent as this celestial brew," he murmured, watching the absinthe cloud into a milky opalescence with the addition of water.

The doctor chuckled, pouring another measure. "There are more things in heaven and earth, Reverend, than are dreamt of in your philosophy," he quipped.

Smythe, his head already light from the potent fumes, ventured a sip and felt the world tilt slightly. The walls, adorned with anatomical sketches and faded battle maps, seemed to breathe. "Truly, Dr. Fletcher, this might just carry us away on heavenly wings."

"Ah, to soar on such wings, beyond the mundane!" Dr. Fletcher exclaimed, his voice becoming increasingly animated. "Consider this our private crusade against the confines of conventional piety and science!"

The night wore on, their conversation a meandering river of philosophical musings and biblical misquotations. Reverend Smythe, his tongue loosened by the spirit's embrace, intoned with theatrical gravitas, "Yea, though I walk through the valley of the shadow, I shall fear no temptation, for this bottle is with me; it comforts and guides me."

As Dr. Fletcher refilled their glasses, his enthusiasm undimmed by the advancing night, he launched into a spirited comparison between their nocturnal experimentations and historic military charges. "You see, Reverend, advancing the frontiers of science with absinthe in hand is akin to leading a cavalry charge—bold, unpredictable, and utterly thrilling!" He gestured expansively toward the shelves lined with bottled creatures, each a silent witness to his scientific forays. "These are my troops, arrayed for battle, and under the influence of our verdant ally here, I've discovered more than in any sober state!"

Reverend Smythe raised his glass as if toasting a hidden congregation. "Each sip unveils layers of prophecy—beasts, dragons, and angels, all swirling in a verdant dance. Imagine John himself, on the isle of Patmos, if he'd had such a libation to illuminate his visions!"

Their laughter echoed through the house, a strange symphony of mirth and madness. As they shared in visions of angels and fairies, science and scripture blurred into a delightful haze, proving that perhaps there was room yet for a middle ground, especially one as delightfully verdant as the one they had found in their glasses.

But, perhaps, dear reader, you are eager to depart from these bacchanalian revels and inquire after other characters scattered across the North York Moors. What, then, of Amelia Rutherford? Her spirits, once so buoyant, now bore the weight of recent tragedies. In the days and weeks following Lord Reginald's funeral, a noticeable shift clouded her demeanor; her once radiant smile dimmed, and her laughter, once a frequent melody in the village, seldom rose above a whisper.

It could be said that the shock of Lord Reginald's untimely demise, compounded by the ghastly revelations concerning poor Molly Dawson, had deeply affected her. Moreover, the abrupt disappearance of Charles Windham, with whom she shared a bond not unnoticed by local gossips, added a poignant solitude to her grief. Charles had vanished soon after liquidating his stable of horses, ostensibly fleeing the looming shadows of his debts and past misdeeds. Rumors abounded that he had fled far from the reach of his creditors, leaving behind unanswered questions and a tangled web of emotions.

Amelia was seen less frequently in the usual social haunts, yet she was occasionally spotted by the rugged coast, gazing pensively out to sea as if she awaited the return of a long-lost ship. There, against the backdrop of relentless waves and under the vast expanse of sky, her silhouette spoke of a melancholy acceptance of her changed fortunes. Yet one must nevertheless hope and expect that a woman of such beauty and with such a fine collection of jewelry will find a path to happiness once more.

Yet what of Harriet Westbrook, our indefatigable purveyor of tales and secrets? In the intricate dance of societal whispers, the very act of weaving narratives from the threads of others' lives may tangle one's own fate in unexpected ways. Unbeknownst to her, the truths she had chanced upon in her enthusiastic sleuthing were indeed correct—she had unwittingly identified the true perpetrator behind the dreadful demise of Lord Reginald. Alas, the full scope of her accuracy would never grace the pages of her eagerly anticipated manuscript, 'Murder at the Manor'. Think of the chapters she could have filled, the rich tapestry of intrigue she could have spun even further!

Though, if such was her punishment, it was a gentle one, cushioned by the bliss of unawareness. She remained cheerfully oblivious to the depth of her own correctness, thus sparing her the torment of what could have been. Her days continued to be filled with the less perilous intrigues of life in the North York

Moors, her ear always inclined to the ground in anticipation of the next great tale. After all, one need not know the entire plot to enjoy the play.

And so we conclude our story where we began—at Ashford Manor. Here, under the pale light of dawn, Thomas Graves, the ever-diligent steward, commences his meticulous morning rounds. At 6:03 AM, he polishes the dining hall's silver, each piece reflecting a legacy of stewardship free from tarnish. By 6:17 AM, he is inspecting the ancestral portraits in the east wing, ensuring Sir Edmund's imposing frame bears no trace of neglect.

Newly among these solemn faces is that of Lord Reginald, whose portrait now resides in this hallowed corridor. His stern blue gaze seems to pierce through the hall, posing silent questions that linger in the air like the morning mist. "Thomas, with your vigilant eye, how did treasures slip away under your watch?" one might imagine him inquiring. Or perhaps, with a lecherous grin, "Where is Molly Dawson, that fetching maid? Send her to me, should you find her." Or even, with a brotherly scorn sharpened by jealousy, "What business has my brother here so frequently?!"

Indeed, as Harriet Westbrook would tell you, Julian Ashford's visits to Ashford Manor have notably increased of late. Lady Eleanor, while appreciating the advantages in estate management of a suitor in the Chief Administrator of Railways and Societal Advancement, is less inclined to ever enter into such a matrimonial alliance. This reality, however, proves slow to dawn upon Julian, whose frequent visits now echo with the subtle tension of unmet expectations and the unspoken anxieties of inheritance and duty. Each journey to the manor, each attempt to secure a future intertwined with Ashford's legacy, leaves him grappling with a blend of ambition and a dawning doubt.

Thomas Graves, immersed in his morning duties, found his strict timetable delightfully disrupted by the spirited sound of young feet hastening down the corridor. Jenny and Emma, with the bright enthusiasm unique to youth, approached him with beaming smiles.

"Mr. Graves!" Jenny called out, her voice bubbling with excitement. "Miss Blythe says we may prepare jams for breakfast. Could you please help us gather what we need?"

Thomas, always endeared by the young ladies' inquisitive spirits, agreed with a warm nod and led them to the still room—a cozy nook within the manor where time seemed to slow, surrounded by rows of herbs, spices, and fruit preserves. The air was rich with the scent of lavender and rosemary, mingling with the sweet promise of sugary delights.

"As you see, ladies, here we have everything your hearts might desire for making jam," Thomas explained as they entered. He pointed to the neatly labeled jars of fruits and the rows of sugar and pectin. "Shall we pick blackberries and raspberries today?" he suggested, knowing well the girls' fondness for these particular fruits.

"Yes, let's!" Emma clapped her hands in delight, her eyes wide with the thrill of culinary adventure.

Jenny, equally thrilled, hurried to gather the necessary jars, her small hands carefully selecting each ingredient. "And we'll need lots of sugar, won't we, Mr. Graves?"

But Thomas had frozen. While surveying the shelves stocked with fruits, sugars, and pectin, his eyes had inadvertently passed over a cluster of dried leaves—pennyroyal, carefully preserved and ominously potent. His heart skipped a beat as memories flooded back with a chilling clarity. He had seen all the signs, beginning with the closed-door secret interludes between Lord Reginald and Molly. He had thought the matter had ended, perhaps Lord Reginald had grown bored with this particular affair, but then Thomas observed the subtle changes in Molly, the early signs of a woman with child—signs he, with his keen observation, could not miss.

Thomas knew that this liaison, if left unchecked, could end tragically for both Molly and the unborn child. At best, they would be quietly cast aside, forgotten remnants of a lord's fleeting fancy. At worst, they could plunge the entire Ashford estate into scandal and disgrace. And so, with a heavy heart veiled under the guise of duty, he remembered preparing a tea infused with the dried pennyroyal leaves. His hands had trembled slightly as he steeped the leaves, the aroma filling the kitchen with its sharp, minty scent—a scent that belied its dangerous intentions.

Offering the tea to Molly that fateful morning, he had believed he was acting to protect the Manor, to shield it from the looming shadow of disgrace. He convinced himself it was mercy, a prevention of greater pain that surely awaited her and her child in a world not kind to the bastards of noblemen.

Now, as flashes of Molly's lifeless body streaked through his mind, mingled with the innocent chatter of Jenny and Emma, a profound sorrow welled up within him. The memory of Molly's vibrant spirit, now forever stilled, clashed with the bitter doubts concerning his own role in her fate.

"What are you doing?" Emma inquired, her youthful curiosity peering into Thomas Graves's momentary distraction. Jenny giggled alongside her sister, "Yeah, did you fall asleep?"

Graves, snapping back to the present, turned to the girls with a theatrical look of guilt. "Oh dear, it appears I've been caught in a most dastardly act," he declared, producing a bag of sugar with a flourish as if pulling a rabbit from a hat. "As atonement for my grievous misdeeds, and in hopes of securing your silence on the matter," he continued, bending down to their level with a conspiratorial wink.

Thomas allowed himself to be drawn into the innocent and expectant blue eyes that gazed up at him. Miss Emma, future lady of this grand manor, stood as a beacon of hope, her youthful brightness a stark contrast to the shadows of the past. Thomas chuckled at her eagerness and nodded in agreement, his spirits lifted by the simple joy of the moment. "Remember, girls," he instructed as he handed each a spoon, "the sweetest jams require a generous hand with sugar. But it's the love we stir in that makes them truly special."

As the gleeful laughter fades away, Thomas alone in the still room harbors the knowledge that sometimes—just sometimes—it's the butler who's done it.

ABOUT THE AUTHOR

James Brennan's passion for Victorian literature and intrigue shines through in his debut novel, *Heathland Hollows*. Inspired by the timeless charm of 19th-century storytelling, he invites readers into a world where the splendor of Victorian society conceals its hidden turmoils. With richly drawn characters and evocative settings, Brennan explores human nature against this grand backdrop, unearthing secrets, desires, and moral dilemmas that resonate with today's readers.

Brennan resides in California with his wife and two daughters.

Printed in Great Britain
by Amazon

43793124R00066